Y0-DDO-713

Nerd Squad

Season 1

Todd Borho

Nerd Squad – Episode 1 - Comedy

Premise: FBI recruits an incompetent tech-support nerd from a local big box electronics store called "Fried Electronics".

Dramatis Personae:

Hubert – Tech support geek that is recruited to spy for the FBI.

Berry – Hubert's balding, domineering boss at the electronics store.

Richard Clapper – The FBI recruiter and handler for Hubert.

Melinda – Hubert's co-worker.

Billy – Hubert's co-worker.

Scene 1

Inside a big box electronics store called "Fried Electronics".......

Berry (yelling from his office chair in a domineering manner): Hey, Melinda! Hubert's not back from his service call yet?

Melinda (sarcastic, yelling back from a spot at the customer service desk): I'm not sure! I forgot to turn his tracking chip on!

Berry: Very funny!

Melinda: I thought so!

Billy walks towards Melinda from his cashier's post and joins the banter.

Billy: Hey, I've got an office pool going right now. 2-to-1 odds Hubert managed to screw up the client's machine worse than it was before.

Berry (thinking): Define screw up.

Melinda: How much is the pool?

Billy: Over 50 so far.

Melinda: What the hell, I'm in. It'll at least give me the illusion that my job is interesting.

Berry: I heard that!

Melinda: I wasn't trying to hide it!

Hubert walks in the main entrance, nearly bumps into a customer, then joins the milieu.

Hubert (approaching Berry): Berry, I've got bad news.

Berry (rolling eyes): Here we go. (sighs) What happened?

Hubert: Well, I had a service call, ya know, to install more RAM on a laptop. It was a nice old lady, and she offered me some hot tea.

Billy (whispering to Melinda): This ought to be ripe.

Hubert: I set the tea next to me while I was working on the laptop, and just as I was about to take my first sip, a giant orange cat leaped at me out of nowhere! (pauses)

Berry: Ok, and?

Hubert: And I spilled the tea on her laptop, which no longer functions.

Melinda: Can you fire him now? I've been waiting for this moment.

Billy: Why? He's the only guy here that is desperate enough to find you attractive.

Berry (leaning back in chair, scratching chin): Hmmm, firing Hubert is tempting.

Hubert: Could you not refer to me in the third person when I'm standing right here please?

Berry: Pay for the laptop out of your own pocket, and I won't fire you.

Hubert: Great, thanks.

Berry: Yet.

A mysterious, middle-aged, paranoid looking, sharp dressed man in a black suit walks in the main entrance to the store and approaches Billy and Melinda. Berry hates customers, so he slams his office door.

Mysterious Man: Hey, is the boss man around?

Melinda (condescending): He sure is! But he avoids customers like the plague, so unless you're here to give him like a million dollars or something, then you have no hope.

Mysterious Man: I'm from the federal government.

Billy (pointing to Berry's office door): That's his office right there!

Mysterious man approaches Berry's door and does a super loud cop knock.

Billy (whispering to Melinda and Hubert in the background): I knew he didn't pay his taxes!

Berry answers the door.

Berry: Hi, I'm Berry, the manager here. That's Berry with an "E". Can I help you?

Mysterious Man: You spell your name like the fruit?

Berry: Helps me stand out.

Mysterious Man: I'm from the federal government, with a capital "G". I need a word with you in private.

They step into Berry's office.

Mysterious Man: I'm FBI Agent Richard Clapper.

Berry (eyes narrowing, twisting lips): Hmmmm, Richard Clapper?

Clapper (impatient): Yeah.

Berry (laughing): Dick Clapper?

Clapper: Like I've never heard that one before.

Berry: Sorry, how can I help you?

Clapper: I'm here to recruit one of your Nerd Squad technicians.

Berry (scratching bald head): Is the FBI that hard up for tech support?

Clapper (sighing): No, not tech support. We need spies. Lots of dangerous villains out there these days after 9/11, ya know.

Berry: Oh, sure. Well, ok, the best and brightest we have to offer is definitely Melinda.

Clapper: Oh, no no. I don't want your best or your brightest.

Berry (confused): Excuse me?

Clapper: No, we prefer borderline morons. It gives us something we call "plausible deniability". Ya know, nobody would ever believe that the FBI would employ a buffoon as a spy. Get it?

Berry (shocked): I guess. (shrugs shoulders) Well, suit yourself. I guess Hubert would be your man.

Clapper: Is that the awkward looking, self-conscious fellow out there?

Berry: You have a well-trained eye.

Clapper: That's strange. Usually guys like that are brilliant behind a keyboard.

Berry: Yeah, usually that's the case. That's what I thought when I hired him. He holds the national corporate record for most failed service calls.

Clapper (exuberant): Perfect! Bring him in here!

Berry slings the door open…..

Berry (yelling): Hey, Hubert! In here, now!

Hubert gulps heavily and his eyes dart around nervously.

Billy (to Melinda): If he goes to prison, then Berry won't have to fire him.

Melinda: This day is looking up.

Hubert walks into the office reluctantly. Berry slams the door. Clapper slaps Hubert on the back and nearly knocks him over.

Clapper: Congratulations! I'm giving you the opportunity of a lifetime, a chance to serve your country and keep it safe from terrorists!

Hubert (looking at Berry): Is this one of your cruel practical jokes, Berry?

Berry: Does it look like I'm laughing?

Clapper: It's no joke, son. The FBI is looking for individuals like yourself to help us keep the country safe. And it pays well, too. What do ya say?

Hubert: Um, well, what would I be doing exactly?

Clapper: Rule number one to working for us, Pubert.

Hubert: Hubert.

Clapper: Oh, sorry, Hubert. Rule number one is to not ask questions. Got it?

Hubert: Will I get a gun?

Clapper (grimacing): That counts as a question, and the answer is now, and always will be, a thunderous no. (puts his arm around Hubert) Come on, what do ya say?

Hubert: Well, yeah, that sounds exciting. I can't wait to tell my friends!

Clapper: Oh no, this is top secret. You can't tell anyone, ok?

Berry: Don't worry. He doesn't have any friends.

Clapper: Perfect!

Hubert: So when do I start?

Clapper: When is your next service call?

Hubert: In an hour. Mr. Puddleston again. Probably an easy fix. Last time he just forgot to plug his desktop in. Silly old man.

Clapper: Excellent. He'll be your first assignment.

Hubert (silly look of uncertainty on his face): Mr. Puddleston? The guy is like 80 years old! How could he possibly be a terrorist?

Clapper: Can't leave any stone unturned, son. The more nondescript they appear, the more dangerous they could be.

Hubert: I'm not sure I can do this. I've been to his house at least ten times. He shared oatmeal with me. We've bonded!

Clapper: You get 500 bucks per assignment.

Hubert (beaming): On second thought, it was crappy oatmeal. I think I'll do it.

Clapper: Great! (turns to Berry) I'm gonna need you to step out for a moment.

Berry: But this is my office!

Clapper glares at him.

Berry: Ok, ok. (walks out and slams door)

Melinda: What's going on, Berry?

Berry: They're making Hubert a spy.

Melinda: What?!

Clapper (yelling from behind the door): I heard that!

Berry: You didn't say that I couldn't say anything!

Clapper (speaking to Hubert): So here's what ya do. It's really simple. You make mental notes of things around his house, anything that might seem suspicious. Then you copy his entire hard drive and report back to me.

Hubert (biting lower lip, having second thoughts): 500 bucks, huh?

Clapper: Cash.

Hubert (holds hand out): Deal!

Clapper shakes Hubert's hand briskly.

Hubert: Ow!

Clapper (handing Hubert a business card): Call me at this number when you're ready to report. I expect to hear from you within 24 hours.

They walk out and find Hubert's co-workers standing around with their arms crossed and beleaguered looks on their faces. Clapper looks around in a paranoid manner a few times quickly, then puts on his shades and leaves the store.

Melinda: Why you!? I'm the best techie here! It's not fair!

Hubert (pompous): I guess the FBI doesn't share your less than expert opinion of yourself, missy.

Billy: He'll blow it.

Hubert (puffing bird-chest out, circling close to Melinda): So now that I'm a spy, I suppose you find me irresistible.

Melinda: Berry, I feel nauseous. Can I go home?

Berry: And miss the excitement? Hubert Bond here has his first assignment in less than an hour. You're not gonna want to miss this!

Billy: Mr. Puddleston? You're going to spy on Mr. Puddleston?

Hubert (nervous): Hey, keep your voice down. You're not even supposed to know.

Billy: Can I go with you? I want to record you screwing up. I figure it should be worth at least a hundred thousand views online.

Hubert (huffing); Berry, I'm taking my lunch now so I can prep for Puddleston, ok?

Berry: Sure, good luck! Be careful! That old man could whip ya in a heartbeat!

Everyone laughs as Hubert walks out.

End Episode 1

Episode 2

Scene 1

Hubert is approaching the humble suburban home of Mr. Puddleston.

Hubert (nervous, mumbling to himself): Oh, my God. What am I doing? I'm a spy. What? I'm spying on Mr. Puddleston. I probably shouldn't be saying this out loud. Nobody can hear me, right?

Hubert gets to the front door and rings the doorbell. After a few moments, he gets impatient and rings it multiple times. Mr. Puddleston finally answers.

Mr. Puddleston (weak, old man voice): Hi, Hubert. Sorry it took me so long to answer. I was in the back yard tending the garden. Come on in.

Hubert: No problem. (wipes sweat from brow, eyes dart around nervously as he makes mental notes of the house)

Mr. Puddleston: You ok?

Hubert (hands shaking): Sure, why do you ask? I'm great. Everything is normal.

Mr. Puddleston: You're sweating and shaking. Did you get beat up again?

Hubert: Don't be silly. That never happens! So what's going on with your machine?

Mr. Puddleston: Take your pick. My blender's on the fritz, too. Couldn't have my morning oatmeal, garlic, banana, and kale smoothie.

Hubert (grim): How awful. I was referring to your desktop computer.

They continue into the living room and approach the computer. Hubert immediately notices that the computer is unplugged, but pretends to not notice so he can get access to the hard drive.

Mr. Puddleston: She won't even boot up. I don't even know why I have the darn thing.

Hubert: To email your grandchildren, right?

Mr. Puddleston (huffy): Yeah, nobody can talk on the phone anymore.

Hubert: Well, I'll take a look and you can get back to your garden.

Mr. Puddleston: I'll watch for a bit. Who knows, maybe I'll learn something.

Hubert (anxious): I wouldn't count on it. Ya know what I could use? Some coffee. Would you mind?

Mr. Puddleston: Coffee maker broke last week. Damn Chinese.

Hubert: Your coffee maker breaking isn't exactly a good reason to belittle well over a billion people. Maybe some scrambled eggs?

Mr. Puddleston: At two in the afternoon?

Hubert (testy): Anything from the kitchen that takes a few minutes to make!

Mr. Puddleston: Corndog?

Hubert: Sure, nuke me a dog. That's great.

Mr. Puddleston walks away. Hubert plugs in the computer, copies the hard drive onto a memory stick, then starts snooping around the room. As he's leaning over a corner table next to a window, he knocks over a vase that shatters into bits. Mr. Puddleston walks in.

Mr. Puddleston: Hubert!

Hubert: I'm so sorry.

Mr. Puddleston: That was my wife's favorite vase!

Hubert (grimacing): I'll make it up to you somehow.

Mr. Puddleston: It's ok. I always hated the thing.

Hubert (surprised and relieved): Ok, well, on the bright side, your computer is running like a champ.

Mr. Puddleston: What was the problem?

Hubert (fumbling for an explanation): Oh, um, it was, ya know, pretty technical.

Mr. Puddleston: You think I'm some sort of dummy?

Hubert: No, not at all. (glances at non-existent watch) I really need to get going. (starts walking to the exit)

Mr. Puddleston: What about the corndog?

Scene 2

Hubert is waiting for his FBI contact, Richard Clapper, on the outer edges of the Fried Electronics parking lot. A black Prious approaches and Clapper gets out, dressed in a black suit, wearing shades, gawking around in a paranoid manner, and holding a briefcase.

Hubert: You drive a Prious?

Clapper: We can't all drive black Mercedes, now can we?

Hubert: Are you really FBI?

Clapper: Watch your mouth, kid. You got the goods?

Hubert: Interesting choice of words. And why a parking lot? Don't you think it looks suspicious?

Clapper: You shouldn't be so paranoid.

Hubert starts to hand the memory stick to Clapper, but then….

Clapper: No! Don't hand it directly to me! Put it in the passenger seat of my car.

Hubert (confused): Okaaay. (puts memory stick on seat)

Clapper: Damn rookies. Ok, so I'm gonna put this briefcase in your car.

Hubert: Ok, then what?

Clapper (rolling eyes): No questions, remember? (puts briefcase in Hubert's old Tokota Tercel)

Hubert just stares at Clapper for a minute.

Clapper: Well, go ahead and open it!

Hubert huffs, opens the briefcase, and finds a thick stack of one dollar bills. He shoves the bills into his glove compartment.

Clapper: Well.

Hubert: What?

Clapper: Gimme the damn briefcase back. (Hubert hands back the case)

Clapper: So what'd you see at the old man's house?

Hubert: Well, he's got a garden.

Clapper (throws hands in air in disgust): I knew it! Damn preppers!

Hubert: He's got a bunch of pictures of his family all over his house.

Clapper: Never trust a man with a big family. Muslims have huge families, ya know.

Hubert: I'm struggling to comprehend the significance of that.

Clapper: You'll learn.

Hubert: He has really disgusting smoothies for breakfast and has tons of furniture from the seventies.

Clapper: Does he have any guns?

Hubert: I didn't see any.

Clapper: Wiley old prepper-terrorist must be hiding his arsenal! Great job, kid! I gotta run!

Clapper hastily gets in his Prious and speeds across the parking lot, nearly hitting a teenager, and drawing general ire from onlookers.

Hubert: What have I gotten into?

Scene 3

Hubert is driving home in the vaunted Kota T-cell....

Hubert (feeling good, winks at self in rear-view mirror): James Bond's got nothin on me.

Police lights suddenly flash behind Hubert......

Hubert: Oh, fudgesickles! (pulls car over)

Cop approaches the old T-cell....

Cop: Do you know why I pulled you over?

Hubert (nervous, runs hand through hair): Umm, well, no.

Cop: You were going 43 in a 40 zone.

Hubert: Is it that time of the month?

Cop (angry): What's that supposed to mean?

Hubert (shaky): Ya know, for quotas.

Cop: Why are you so nervous?

Hubert: Cuz I don't like police.

Cop: What?!

Hubert: I mean, um, geez. Cops just make me nervous. I'm sorry.

Cop: I'm gonna need to search your vehicle. Please step out.

Hubert gets out and stands by as the cop rummages though his stuff. He opens the glove box and a giant pile of ones falls out.

Cop: Hmmm, that's interesting. Why so much money, and in small bills?

Hubert (eyes rolling in back of head, trying to think of good excuse): Would you believe me if I told you I was a stripper?

Cop (huffing): This looks awful bad, kid. I'll tell ya what I'm gonna do, though. You seem decent, so I'll let ya off the hook, but I can't let you go on with a pile of cash like that.

Hubert (frowning): You can't?

Cop: Nope, I'll just take it and be on my way.

Hubert: I'm not getting a ticket?

Cop (grinning): Nope, it's your lucky day.

Scene 4

The next day at Fried Electronics, Hubert walks in and is greeted by his milieu.....

Billy: Did the FBI fire you yet?

Hubert: Not yet.

Billy frowns and hands 20 bucks to Melinda.

Melinda: So how'd it go at Mr. Puddleston's?

Hubert: You know I can't talk about that.

Melinda (hands on hips): Oooo, look at big mister top secret!

Billy: So whatcha gonna do with all that cash? Make a down payment on a new and improved clunker?

Hubert (sighing deeply): Well, that might be jumping the gun a bit. I don't have the money.

Melinda (laughing): You didn't get paid? You got ripped off by the FBI?

Hubert: No, they paid me, but I got pulled over on my way home.

Billy: So?

Hubert: So that paranoid psycho, Dick Clapper, paid me with 500 one dollar bills. The cop said it was suspicious, so he took it.

Billy (laughing with arms folded): Just remember, there's a lesson to be learned here.

Hubert: Oh yeah. What's that?

Billy: Damned if I know.

The Nerd Squad manager, Berry, opens his office door and yells....

Berry: Hubert! Get in here!

Hubert walks in, hunched over and dejected.

Berry: How'd your first mission go?

Hubert: Can't say.

Berry: Right. Top secret. So your freak boss from the FBI called.

Hubert: Ok, whatsup?

Berry: He wants you to call him.

Hubert (confused): Why didn't you just put me on the line with him?

Berry: He said it wasn't a secure line or some mumbo jumbo. He said to call him from a pay phone.

Hubert (wrinkling nose, shocked): What? Do those even still exist?

Berry: Yes, they do. And yes, I'm that old.

Hubert: Where can I find one?

Berry: Actually, he gave me specific directions to a particular pay phone he wants you to use.

Hubert: This isn't worth the money.

Berry: He also said not to send the directions to you electronically, so here's a crumpled piece of paper with my scribble.

Hubert takes the paper and squints at it for a moment, trying to decipher the scribble.

Hubert: This is all the way on the other side of town!

Berry: And I'll have to dock your pay while you're gone.

Scene 5

Hubert has a phone in his hand at a phone booth in a sketchy neighborhood....

Clapper: Good news, kid. Mr. Prick is happy with your work and is ready to give you another job.

Hubert: Who's Mr. Prick?

Clapper: My boss.

Hubert: Should you be telling me that?

Clapper: Probably not. Anyway, there's a person of interest we got from Mr. Puddleston's files. I'll be into Fried Electronics tomorrow to talk it over with you.

Hubert: You made me drive all the way to a pay phone, and then you give away the location of our meetings?

Clapper: Good point. Oh well. I'll see ya tomorrow.

Hubert (sarcastically): Can't wait. (slams receiver down in disgust)

An unsavory character approaches Hubert.

Unsavory Character: Hey dude.

Hubert tries to walk away.

Unsavory Character: That your ride?

Hubert: Yep, that's my old beast.

Unsavory Character: Tell ya what. I'll let ya keep it for 20 bucks.

Hubert reaches in pocket and pulls out 20.

Hubert: That's all I've got.

Unsavory Character: Not true. You've got this rolling junk pile.

End Episode 2

Episode 3

Scene 1

Back at Nerd Squad headquarters inside Fried Electronics department store…..Hubert walks in and finds Clapper waiting for him, casually twirling in a puffy office chair.

Clapper: Hey Hubert. Nice striped shirt! Wow, I didn't think it was possible, but it actually makes you look skinnier.

Hubert (looking at himself in self-conscious manner): Well, what do you want, that I dress in all black like a cat burglar or something?

Clapper: Not criticizing, just analyzing.

Hubert: You're here awfully early. Where's Berry?

Berry's voice comes from his personal office in back, with the door shut….

Berry (shouting): I'm in here, guzzling coffee, eavesdropping, and wondering where my life went wrong!

Clapper (shouting back): I thought you said you couldn't hear from in there!

Berry: You bought that?! You're not very good at your job!

Clapper (turns back to Hubert): Ok, kid. Here's your next assignment. We found a guy on Puddleston's email list that we want you to get at. His name is Mohamed Jones.

Hubert: So what did he do?

Clapper: Well, he's Muslim.

Hubert: And?

Clapper: Do you need another reason?

Berry (yelling behind his door): I'm scared of Muslims!

Clapper: The tricky part is, he's never been a customer here.

Hubert: So how the hell am I supposed to get into his house?

Clapper: You're reasonably smart. Can't you infect his computer with a virus or something?

Berry: Don't overestimate him!

Melinda and Billy walk into the picture.

Clapper: You two aren't privy to this conversation, so I'm gonna have to ask you to leave.
Melinda (groggy): I work here, unfortunately. You don't.

Berry (yelling): It's ok, you guys come in here and eavesdrop with me!

Hubert (excited): Wait, I got it! Melinda can do it!

Melinda: I'm not doing anything that you think is a good idea.

Billy: I don't blame you.

Clapper: No way, kid.

Hubert: Why not?

Clapper: Cuz she's not on the payroll.

Hubert: So put her on the payroll!

Melinda: I'm listening.

Clapper: You guys gotta go.

Melinda: I'm declaring myself privy to this conversation. What am I getting paid for?

Clapper: You're not!

Berry (comes out of office): Spying on a Muslim. You gotta somehow get Hubert into his house in a quasi-legitimate way.

Billy: A Muslim? That's simple. Just show him some ankle, Melinda.

Clapper (scribbling furiously on notepad, then rips sheet off and hands to Hubert): Here's his address and all the info you need, kid. I'm leaving it in your hands. (flustered) If you screw this up, there'll be consequences!

Clapper leaves the building hastily.

Melinda: So I want a 60 percent cut.

Hubert: I'm perfectly capable of doing this alone. And why 60? It should be 50/50.

Berry: Hey, if you're doing this on company time, I'm gonna need at least 20 percent.

Hubert (flustered): What? No, I'll do it on my own time.

Billy (laughing): You're just gonna show up at some random dude's house and convince him to let you in. Not only let you in, but get onto his personal computer?

Hubert (proud, defiant): Yep!

Billy: Great, I'll start the office pool right now. This is gonna be epic!

Berry: Hey, while you're at it, Billy, run across the street to Happy's Bar and see if the staff wants in!

5 minutes later……Hubert is sitting in his old Tokota Tercel, unsure what to do.

Hubert: Hmmm, maybe I'll try calling first, rather than in person. (looks at phone, takes deep breath, dials number)

Phone ringing…..

Mohamed: Hello?

Hubert (nervous, fumbling for words): Hi, you don't have an accent.

Mohamed: Who is this?

Hubert: Oh, um, this is Hubert from Fried Electronics Nerd Squad. We're offering free computer tune-ups.

Mohamed: I hate Fried Electronics. Don't call again. (click)

Hubert (sweating): Glad that wasn't in person.

5 minutes later…Hubert walks back into the office…..

Billy (sarcastic): Hubert! Epically astonished to see you back so soon!

Melinda: I should raise my cut to 70.

Hubert: Ok, ok, 60 percent, and you can't tell Clapper. Deal?

Melinda: Deal. You get paid 500, right?

Hubert: Yep.

Melinda: What's 60 percent of 500?

Billy: More than you make here in a week.

Berry: I still want my 20 percent, too.

Hubert: So I'm risking my neck and making the same amount as you, Berry? How is that fair?

Berry (nonchalant, uncaring): It's not.

Scene 2

Melinda is approaching Mohamed's modest, well-maintained house in the suburbs. She's dressed to impress. Hubert is waiting in his Tercel around the corner. Melinda knocks at front door.

Mohamed (pleasant, smiling): Can I help you?

Melinda: Hi, I'm from Computers-R-Us. We're offering a free computer check-up and free maintenance for six months.

Mohamed: Sure, sounds great! Come on in!

Melinda: I'll send someone over right away.

Mohamed frowns as Melinda walks away.

2 minutes later, Hubert is knocking on the door....

Mohamed: Can I help you?

Hubert: I'm Hubert, from Computers-R-Us.

Mohamed: What happened to the girl?

Hubert: She's just in sales. I'm the tech guy.

Mohamed: Bummer. (rolls eyes) Come in, I guess.

As they walk through the house, Hubert notices a handsome, fully stocked gun rack. He also sees some bacon strips on the kitchen table.

Hubert: I thought Muslims don't eat pork.

Mohamed (surprised): What makes you think I'm Muslim?

Hubert (grasping for words): Oh, I dunno. Just, ya know.

Mohamed: Because of my name?

Hubert: Maybe.

Mohamed: I'm not Muslim, and I've never even visited a so-called Muslim country. (gestures to the desk and computer) Have a seat.

Hubert sits. Mohamed stares at him.

Hubert: Could I have some water?

Mohamed (suspicious): I'm sorry, I don't feel comfortable leaving you alone. You can come with me to the kitchen if you want.

Hubert: On second thought, this will only take a few minutes. I'll be ok. (digs out cell phone from pocket) Gotta contact work real quick.

Hubert sends a text to Melinda and asks for her to come knock again. A few minutes later, there's a loud bang on the door.

Mohamed: I'll be back, fast.

Mohamed opens front door.

Melinda: Hey, sorry, me again. I got a flat tire, can you help me real quick? My car is just around the corner.

Mohamed: I suppose I could take a look.

Hubert takes the opportunity to copy Mohamed's hard drive. Mohamed returns.

Hubert: All finished up!

Mohamed: Your sales girl's car got stolen.

Hubert (feigning shock): Oh no!

Mohamed: She's outside crying.

Hubert: Ok, well, I'd better get going. Your computer is in tip-top shape.

Mohamed: Where is your store located?

Hubert: Um, downtown. I'll email you.

Mohamed: Do you need my email address?

Hubert: Nope, already got it.

Mohamed: I didn't give it to you.

Hubert: Ya didn't? Well, then, I'd better get it.

Mohamed (suspicious): On second thought, let me get your contact info as well.

They swap contact info. Hubert leaves.

Scene 3

The next day at Nerd Squad headquarters in Fried Electronics......

Melinda: So Hubert gave him his real name and contact info.

Billy (laughing): This surprises you?
Melinda: It does, but it shouldn't.

Berry: Where is that little pip-squeak, anyway?

Melinda: Hopefully collecting our money.

Scene 4

Hubert is talking with Clapper at a park.

Clapper (laughing): You gave him your real name?

Hubert: Is that a problem?

Clapper: For you, it might be. Not for me, that's why I'm laughing.

Hubert: So when's my next assignment?

Clapper: After we dig through this Muslim guy's data, we'll find someone for ya.

Hubert: He's not even Muslim, ya know.

Clapper (paranoid, looking over shoulder): That's what he'd like us to think.

Scene 5

The next day, Clapper is in the office of his boss, Mr. Prick, at FBI headquarters.

Mr. Prick (pacing around anxiously): Wow, a Muslim with guns, a garden, and has contact with an anarchist.

Clapper (shaking head): What is this world coming to, sir?

Mr. Prick (slams fist on desk, dark red face): Dammit, Clapper, isn't it obvious?! It's a damn Anarcho-Muslim Gun And Garden Network!

Clapper (scratching chin thoughtfully): Hmmmm, that's a hell of an acronym, sir. AMGAGN. It's just so crazy, it might be right!

Mr. Prick (hands on hips): Dammit, Clapper, of course it's right! I thought of it, didn't I?

Clapper: I can't argue with that flawless logic, sir. The question is, what do we do now?

Mr. Prick: You send the kid after this anarchist girl, that's what! She'll lead us up the ladder to the AMGAGN leadership!

Clapper: Are you sure you want to use such an incompetent asset on a high value target, sir?

Mr. Prick (slams hand on desk again): Dammit, Clapper! Of course. The more incompetent, the more plausible deniability he gives us. We need results, Clapper! Now get on it!

Clapper (standing and saluting): Yes, sir!

End Episode 3

Episode 4

Scene 1

Hubert is meeting Clapper in a deserted parking lot.

Hubert: Don't you think this is a little cliché? I mean, who really meets like this?

Clapper: Dammit, Pubert. You need to be more paranoid if you're gonna survive in this game.

Hubert: HUBERT!

Clapper: What? Oh, right.

Hubert: Whatever. Can we hurry this up. If I'm late for work again, Berry's gonna blackmail me again.

Clapper (feigning sympathy): Awww, geeee, I'm so sorry. Is your little dead end job at an electronics store more important than national security? Does it say in your contract that I'm not allowed to make you late for work?

Hubert (confused): I didn't sign a contract.

Clapper: Damn right! And don't you forget it!

Hubert: You make zero sense.

Clapper: Welcome to government work, kid. Ok, so anyway, stop distracting me. Down to business. So your next target is a known anarchist. We need to get the goods on her so she'll lead us up the chain of command. Here's her name and address.

Hubert (mouth gapes open as he glances at the paper): Holy socks and underwear.

Clapper: What's the problem, kid?

Hubert: I know this girl.

Clapper: You do?! How can a scrawny twerp like you know such a knockout?

Hubert: She lives in my building.

Clapper: Really? Great!

Hubert (uncertain): I guess.

Clapper: Now you've got an excuse to talk to her. Don't blow it, kid. Your country is counting on you.

Scene 2

Nerd Squad headquarters at Fried Electronics. Hubert walks in 5 minutes late after his meeting with Clapper.

Berry (excited, pointing to his watch): Hubert! You're late! You know the drill.

Hubert (sighing, shrugging shoulders): Yeah, yeah. You get five percent of my next FBI gig so you won't fire me.

Berry: The way you say it makes it sound so wrong.

Hubert: It is wrong!

Berry: Hey, I've got bills just like everybody else.

Billy: So Hubert, who's your next unsuspecting victim?

Hubert: You know I can't tell you.

Billy (stroking handlebar mustache): Oh, come on Hubert, you know I can't get the office betting pool going if we don't at least have some details.

Melinda: That's not true. You could just have a basic bet like success or failure. Ya know, like red or black.

Billy: Good point. But it's so much more exciting if we can make multiple bets.

Melinda: Come on Hubert. I'll make out with you if you tell us.

Hubert: You think I'm that gullible?

Billy (to Melinda): You think he's that desperate?

Melinda kicks Billy in the shin.

Scene 3

Hubert is driving his Tokota Tercel on his way to his apartment building to fulfill his mission.

Hubert (nervous): What am I doing? This is crazy. Maybe I should just ask her out and quit my FBI gig. No, that's even crazier. Maybe I should just drive around aimlessly for a while and think about it. No, be a man. You got this!

Hubert parks in his usual spot.

20 minutes later, Hubert is still sitting in his car…..

Hubert: Dammit, what's wrong with me? (slaps himself in the face) What's wrong with you? (slaps himself in the face again)

A woman with a concerned look on her face walks by, watching Hubert slap himself in the face, shaking her head disapprovingly. They make eye contact.

Hubert (yelling out window): What! You've never seen a crazy guy before!?

Woman runs away.....

Hubert takes a deep breath and steps out. As he's walking slowly towards the apartment of his target, he coincidentally runs into her (literally) as he rounds the corner, and spills her drink.

Hubert: OH! I'm so sorry!

Sophia (brushing herself off, laughing): It's ok. I like wearing iced mocha.

Hubert: You do? Why?

Sophia: It was a joke. Hey, don't I know you from somewhere?

Hubert (starting to sweat, shaking head slowly): Nope. Total strangers.

Sophia: Hmmm, no. Wait, I got it! Yeah, you live here in the building!

Hubert: I do?

Sophia: Yeah, yeah, you're that guy that always looks so afraid when we cross paths. You freak out and scurry away.

Hubert: Scurry?

Sophia: Yep, I'm sure it's you. You do live here. (holds out hand) I'm Sophia. No need to scurry.

Hubert (shakes her hand): I'm Hubert.

Sophia: Wow, your hand is sweaty. Do you always sweat this much?

Hubert: No, well, ya see, I just got done working out.

Sophia (skeptically): Really? You work out?

Hubert: Yep. I'm a huge gym rat. Actually, I'm on my way to the gym right now.

Sophia (confused): Didn't you say you just finished?

Hubert: Um, did I?

Sophia: Yep. Well, anyway, I'm gonna go get another iced mocha. I'll see ya around, ok?

Hubert: Yeah, I hope so.

Scene 4

Later that day at Happy's Bar, across the street from Fried Electronics, the Nerd Squad is having some after work cocktails, minus Hubert. Hubert doesn't usually drink. Happy, the bar owner, tends the bar. He's tall, husky, wears skin tight clothes, and has a deep, raspy voice.

Melinda: So Mr. Clobberhead accused us today of sabotaging his equipment just so we get more business! Can you guys believe that?

Billy and Berry in unison (with deadpan faces): Yeah.

Melinda: Why do you say that?

Billy: Cuz I sabotaged his equipment.

Berry: And I told Billy to sabotage his equipment.

Happy: You guys wouldn't do that to my system, would ya?

Billy: Nah. We don't mess with people who can easily crush us.

Berry (nodding in agreement): Or who gives us free drinks.

Hubert walks in and approaches the group at the bar.

Happy: Are you lost?

Berry: How'd your FBI gig go today?

Billy: It went terrible. Why do you think he's at a bar?

Melinda: You assume too much, Billy. He hasn't even had any drinks.

Happy sets a huge glass of scotch in front of Hubert. Hubert slams it in a few gulps.

Melinda: I hate to say it, Billy, but you were right.

Hubert slouches into a barstool.

Berry: So who's your target? Come on, we're at a bar. Your secrets are safe here.

Hubert (pouty face): My neighbor who I've had a crush on for years.

Billy: Ouch, that hurts. Double fail, huh? You didn't get your target, and you didn't get the girl.

Hubert: I went this afternoon.

Berry: And ya chickened out.

Hubert: I ran into her.

Melinda: And?

Hubert: I literally ran into her and spilled her coffee. It was such dumb luck.

Happy (sarcastically): Are you a stranger to dumb luck, Hubert?
Billy: So you apologized and offered to replace the drink, right?

Hubert: Um, no.

Billy (facepalm): Man, that was your in! You could've had a date, completely by accident!

Melinda: That wouldn't be what I'd classify as a date.

Berry: I think for Hubert that would count.

Melinda (looking Hubert up and down): You've got a point.

Happy (pouring another glass of scotch): Hey, look on the bright side, Hubert. She's your neighbor, knows you exist, so the next meeting will be less awkward. (points to glass) This one is on me.

Hubert slams the double shot of scotch and starts to wobble. He jumps at the sound of his phone.

Hubert (slurring speech): Hey Clapper.

Clapper: Hubert! You were supposed to make contact after that thing you were supposed to do today!

Hubert: You mean my mission? Um, yeah, about that.

Clapper: Dammit, Hubert, don't say mission on the phone! This is sensitive stuff!

Billy (yelling): Epic fail! Abort!

Clapper: Hubert, what the hell was that? Where are you?

Hubert (slurring)· Just, just, ya know, finishing work. (giggles)

Clapper: You sound drunk! Are you at a bar?

Berry (yelling and giggling): Lie, Hubert, lie!

Clapper: Is that Berry's voice? You didn't tell them about that thing, did you?

Hubert: The scotch made me do it.

Clapper: You're on thin ice, buddy.

Hubert: Ice? No, I drank it straight up.

Clapper: Sober up and get it done, Hubert. I want a full report ASAP. (hangs up)

Happy sets the entire bottle of scotch in front of Hubert.

Happy: Ya know, if ya drink enough of this stuff, there's a chance you won't remember any of this tomorrow.

End Episode 4

Episode 5

Scene 1

Hubert is leaning on the customer service counter at Nerd Squad headquarters in Fried Electronics. He has a mopey face.

Melinda: Stop moping around.

Billy: The guy has no life. Give him a break.

Berry (yelling from manager's office, sitting in head honcho chair): Hey, can you guys at least look like you're working!

Billy: NO!

Berry: Ok, just doing my job! Carry on!

Hubert: Isn't anyone going to ask why I'm moping around?

Melinda: Nah, probably not. But go ahead and tell us anyway.

Billy: I know why. You don't even need to say it. You haven't had the huevos to go spy on your hot neighbor yet.

Berry (yelling from office): Obvious!

Melinda: Why don't you just come out here if you want to talk to us?!

Berry: Because I like yelling!

Hubert: I'm gonna do it tonight. I've gotta do something so Clapper will get off my ass.

Melinda: Watch how you phrase things.

Billy: Can I come?

Hubert (offended): Um, no.

Billy: Come on, maybe it'll help take the edge off.

Hubert (rubbing neck): There is no edge.

Billy: Whatever you say, man. Hey, I've got a great idea. Why don't you film it and put it on youtube. Make the most of your futile effort.

Hubert (offended, scoffs): Not futile, and not filming.

Billy: Can I film it?

Hubert twists face and gives sideways glance.

Scene 2

Hubert is pacing around his apartment complex trying to work up the nerve to approach Sophia. Billy is lurking in the bushes, waiting to film with his phone.

Billy (thinking to himself): Does what I'm doing right now make my life more pathetic than his?

Hubert starts walking towards Sophia's door. Billy starts filming. A pigeon poops on Hubert's shoulder. Hubert screams and runs to his apartment to change shirts. Billy starts dreaming of what to do with the money he'll make from the video.

A few minutes later, Hubert emerges in a fresh shirt, approaches Sophia's door, and knocks.

Sophia: Hi. Hubert, right?

Hubert: Yep, that's me.

Awkward silence…..

Sophia: How do you know which apartment I live in?

Hubert: You told me.

Sophia: I'm pretty sure I didn't.

Hubert: You're right, I'm sorry, I followed you.

Sophia: Wow, that's not creepy. So what brings you by?

Hubert: Um, actually, my company is offering a great deal on computer maintenance service right now and I thought you might be interested.

Sophia: Really? What's the deal?

Hubert: Um, free maintenance for life.

Sophia: Wow, that sounds too good to be true!

Hubert: OH, I mean, um, for six months. Just six months. I mean, I would service you for life, but I'm not sure the company would appreciate that.

Sophia (grimacing, sarcastic): You sure do have a way with words. Anyway, sure, come on in.

Hubert enters. Billy's jaw drops from shock. He approaches the window and is pleased to find a crack where he can get audio and video.

Hubert gawks around and notices a huge, packed bookshelf lining the wall. He also notices there is no TV.

Hubert: You don't have a TV?

Sophia (amused): No, I read books instead. Do you read?

Hubert: Not since high school.

Sophia (sour face): I see. Anyway, the laptop is over there on the desk, so go ahead and do your thing.

Hubert takes a seat at the desk and Sophia disappears into another room. She reappears and takes a seat on the sofa, near Hubert. She starts casually cleaning a handgun. Noticing this, Hubert does a double take, his eyes start bulging from his head, and he starts hyperventilating.

Sophia: Are you ok?

Hubert (gasping, barely able to talk): G, gu, gu, gun! Why do you have a g..g...gun?

Sophia (cheerful): For self-defense, of course. I thought I'd clean it while you're working.

Hubert: Um, ok, guns kind of make me nervous. Could you do it in another room?

Sophia (laughing): Why do guns make you nervous?

Hubert: Because they kill people.

Sophia: Guns don't kill people. Immoral people murder people. (noticing Hubert's hands trembling) But I guess if you're gonna get any work done, I'll have to put the gun away. (she stashes it in a drawer in the coffee table)

Hubert: Could you actually put it in another room?

Sophia: Sure thing.

She takes the gun and walks out. Hubert takes the opportunity to start copying her hard drive to his external disk. Sophia comes back.

Hubert: So may I ask what you do?

Sophia: You mean to earn slave survival credits?

Hubert: Um, what?

Sophia: Money.

Hubert: Yep.

Sophia: Why is that the first question people always ask? Anyway, I do a lot. I'm a freelance writer and photographer. I sell 3D printed objects. I trade cryptos.

Hubert: Cryptos?

Sophia: What century are you in? Cryptocurrency. Like Bitcoin.

Hubert: Oh, right.

Sophia: The best part of all the things I do to "make money", is that it's all extortion-free.

Hubert (confused): Aren't most people's jobs extortion free?

Sophia: No, most people pay taxes. Taxes are a form of extortion.

Hubert (aghast, nearly speechless): I've never heard that before.

Their conversation is interrupted by a howl of anguish coming from outside. They both run to the window to take a look. Billy is screaming and running to desperately get away from a dog.

Hubert: Billy?

Sophia: You know that guy?

Hubert: Unfortunately.

Sophia: What's he doing here?

Hubert (shrugs shoulders): I can only imagine. Maybe you should get that gun.

Sophia: Must be a good friend.

Hubert: Well, I just realized that I need to bring more equipment to do more work on your PC. Can I come back another time?

Sophia: Sure, anytime. And maybe after you're done, I'll take you to the gun range for target practice.

Scene 3

The next day at Fried Electronics Store, Berry, Billy, and Melinda are gathered around one of the big screen displays, when Hubert walks in…..

Hubert: Hey guys, what's going on?

Berry (slaps Hubert on the back): Congratulations, Hubert, you've made it to the big time!

Hubert looks at the screen and is mortified to see a spliced up video featuring himself getting pooped on by a pigeon.

Melinda: The look of absolute degradation on your face is priceless, Hubert! How much money have you made, Billy?

Billy: I've got over a hundred thousand views on youtube, so I dunno, but it's a lot more than I make working here!

Hubert (offended tone): What about the video of you screaming and running away from a dog?

Melinda (intrigued): Dog? Do tell.

Hubert: I've never seen anyone flee from a chihuahua before.

Billy: Not a chihuahua.

Hubert: And I told you not to film!

Billy: Ok, number one, you didn't say no. You just gave a sideways glance. And secondly, to your credit, I had to splice lots of video together to even make it entertaining. I thought you'd blow it so bad that it would speak for itself! But nope, you surprised me. You didn't choke at all. I think she might actually like you.

Berry and Melinda get shocked looks on their faces.

Berry: This is a real girl?

Billy: Yep.

Melinda: Too bad when she finds out you're spying on her for the FBI she's gonna turn into a real killer.

Scene 4

Hubert is meeting Clapper in a deserted parking lot.

Hubert: Couldn't we meet at a coffee shop or something? This is ludicrous.

Clapper: We can't be too careful. By the way, your little youtube video sensation is great and I couldn't stop laughing, but we can't have that happening while you're on FBI time.

Hubert: It wasn't even me! Billy did it!

Clapper: Well, next time be more careful, and if you see anyone filming you, take the proper actions to make them stop.

Hubert: Like what?

Clapper: I find that kicks to the groin tend to be rather convincing. So anyway, about your target. Did you get proof that she's an anarchist?

Hubert: Um, no. Was that what I was supposed to do? I thought I just had to copy her hard drive.

Clapper (facepalming): Ya got a lot to learn kid. No. The hard drive is just the tip of the iceberg. If she's an anarchist, then we'll really have something on our hands. I need you to get proof that she's an anarchist.

Hubert: How am I supposed to do that?

Clapper: Figure it out, kid! Hell, I don't care! Plant something on her, if ya have to! All I know is my boss is breathing down my neck about this, and I need proof, fabricated or not, that this girl is an anarchist.

Hubert (distrustful face): But if it's fabricated, then that means it's not true, right?

Clapper: In our business, it doesn't matter. Let me ask ya this. Does she have any guns?

Hubert: Yeah, actually, and she's pretty open about it.

Clapper (excited): I knew it! Well, that's a start. You can't trust anyone with a gun, kid.

Hubert: But you carry a gun.

Clapper: Yeah, but, I'm government.

Hubert: That seems contradictory

Clapper: Whatever, kid. Did you notice anything else unusual about her?

Hubert: Well, she doesn't have a TV and she has tons of books.

Clapper: Worse than I thought! Damn book readers! You're hot on her trail, kid! Good work. I gotta run. Remember, this meeting never happened!

Hubert: Wait! What about the money!?

Clapper (rolling eyes, patronizing tone): Oh, sure, ya want your money. Here ya go, all ones, just the way you like it. (hands a crinkled paper sack full of bills to Hubert)

Clapper does some quick, paranoid glances in various directions, then scampers off to his car, which is parked on the far side of the empty lot.

Hubert: You should have parked closer!

Clapper: I don't know you!

End Episode 5

Episode 6

Scene 1

At Nerd Squad headquarters in Fried Electronics store, Billy is staring at the wall with a laptop nearby. A male customer is trying to get his attention.

Customer: Excuse me!

Billy continues staring at wall.

Customer: What the hell is wrong with you!?

Billy doesn't budge. Customer leaves in frustration just as Melinda comes in for her shift.

Melinda: Hey, you know a customer just walked out?

Billy (continuing to stare at wall): They're not a customer unless they actually buy something.

Melinda: Yeah, I don't really care, just thought I'd ask. Why are you staring at the wall?

Billy: I'm watching paint dry.

Melinda (notices one square of fresh paint on the wall): Dare I ask why?

Billy: I'm trying to win a bet. I found a website, bet-on-anything dot com, where you can bet on anything. So I'm in the middle of a wager right now with people all around the world.

Melinda: So the bet is on who can watch paint dry the longest?

Billy: Nothing gets past you.

Melinda: Couldn't someone just play a looped video and win every time?

Billy (slowly gets shocked frown, turns away from wall): That didn't occur to me.

Hubert walks in for his shift.

Hubert: Hi guys. (peers into Berry's office) Where's Berry?

Billy: Over at Happy's having some day drinks.

Melinda: Again?

Billy: It's not like he really has to function to do his job. He just sits in his office all day and yells at us occasionally. Hell, the alcohol might actually help with the yelling part.

Melinda: Hubert, you look concerned.

Billy: He always looks like that.
Melinda: No, more than normal.

Hubert: Yeah, I just needed some advice from Berry, that's all.

Billy and Melinda laugh heartily.

Billy: Advice on what? How to sit in a chair 60 hours a week and miraculously avoid the chiropractor?

Hubert: I just wanted a little advice about women.

Billy and Melinda laugh again, almost on the verge of tears.

Melinda: That's funny on so many levels, I don't even know where to begin!

Billy: And I'm kind of offended. I've got loads of experience with the ladies.

Melinda: Talking to cashiers and waitresses doesn't count, Billy.

Billy: Why not?

Melinda: Because they have to talk to you.

Hubert: It's just that Berry used to be married, so I thought he might know a thing or two.

Melinda: Key words here are "used to". Maybe we can help?

Billy: Or if not, at least have more laughs.

Hubert: Ok, ok. Sophia asked me to go to the gun range with her.

Billy: A hot girl asked YOU out? When did I enter this alternate universe? (looking up towards the heavens) I demand answers!

Melinda: So you're gonna go, right?

Hubert: Well, yeah, probably. I just don't know what she's thinking. Like is she thinking it's just a friendly little friend thing, or something else?

Billy: Have you pondered the possibility that maybe she wants to shoot you and make it look like an accident?

Berry walks in.

Berry (slightly slurring): Hey guys! I miss anything?

Melinda: Billy ignored a customer until he got boiling angry and stomped out.

Billy: Total exaggeration. There was no stomping.

Berry: So everything is normal.

Melinda: No, absolutely not normal. Hubert's got a date!

Berry: What?! (eyes roll upwards) Wow, how much did I drink?

Hubert: And another thing is, should I tell Clapper about this?

Melinda: Will he pay you if you do?

Hubert: Yeah, I guess.

Berry slouches into a chair.

Berry: So let me get this straight. You have a chance to get paid for going on a date with a beautiful woman?

Hubert (face perks up): Hmmmm, I didn't think of it like that.

Billy starts banging head against wall.

Melinda: Billy, what the hell?

Billy (shaky, fearful voice): I'm trying to make it stop! This must be a bad dream!

Melinda: Look, Hubert, what have you got to lose? If it goes well with Sophia, you win. If you get shot and die, everybody wins. It's a win-win situation.

Hubert (cringing): Thanks for the pep talk. (sighs) Ok, I'm gonna do it. I'm gonna call Clapper right now.

Melinda: Don't you need to actually set up the date with Sophia first?

Hubert (as he's dialing his phone): She said she's going to the gun range tonight anyway, so I'm sure it'll be fine.

Hubert: Hey, Clapper.

Clapper: I told you not to use my name on the phone. Whatsup, kid?

Hubert: I'm going to the gun range with Sophia. Just thought I'd drop that on ya.

Clapper (pumped up): Wow, kid! This is huge! A gun range! You're really getting in deep! We gotta meet before you go, though, ok?

Billy (yelling): Hey clap-man!

Clapper: Dammit! Is that Billy? Are you calling me from work? This is top secret! What the hell are you thinking?

Hubert: Oh, come on. Everyone here knows I work for the FBI, and they all know you, too.

Clapper: Your sloppiness is getting intolerable, kid! Luckily for you, you're turning out to be quite the valuable asset, so I can overlook some of your reckless behavior.

Hubert: How many assets do you have?

Clapper: Right now, only you, but that's not the point. I'll call ya back within the hour with instructions for the meeting.

Scene 2

Richard Clapper is pacing around a lobby of a 3-star hotel while he waits for Hubert. He is approached by a female member of the staff.

Female Hotel Worker: Can I help you, sir?

Clapper (wearing sunglasses indoors): No thanks, I don't want any.

Worker: What? Are you a guest here at the hotel, sir?

Clapper: Just waiting for a friend of a friend.

Worker (suspicious): I see. Is your friend a hotel guest?

Clapper: He will be.

Worker (not convinced): Sure thing.

The female staff member walks over to the front desk and starts whispering in the ear of another staff member, who gives a disapproving look and starts shaking his head. Hubert walks in the main entrance and approaches Clapper.

Hubert: Wow, swanky. Sure beats the empty parking lot we normally meet at. Do you have a room here?

Clapper (speaking in a low tone): Of course not. I can't afford a place like this. We've gotta hurry. They're onto us.

Hubert (confused): Who's they?

Clapper: The staff.

Hubert facepalms and sighs deeply.

Clapper: Ok, let's hurry. Into the bathroom. (grabs Hubert's arm and starts leading him)

Hubert (shocked): What? Whoa! Why?

Clapper (indignant): You've really gotta stop asking questions, kid.

Two members of the staff take notice and cut them off before they reach the bathroom door.

Worker: Would one of you be kind enough to tell me which room you're staying in?

Clapper (screechy, frantic shout): They're onto us! Run, kid!

Clapper runs away and Hubert follows awkwardly behind.

All staff and guests shake their heads disapprovingly. Clapper and Hubert run down the street and duck into a diner. They're both gasping for air.

Waitress: You boys ok?

Clapper (to waitress): Coffee please. (to Hubert) In the bathroom, now.

Waitress cringes. Clapper and Hubert go into the men's room.

Hubert: What the hell is going on? I don't need 500 dollars this badly!

Clapper: Calm down, kid. I just needed a private spot to get you wired up. (he pulls out a spy wire from his duffel bag) Now lift up your shirt.

Hubert: Wire? Why do I need a wire?

Clapper: Use your imagination kid. I want everything documented that happens with you and that anarchist at the gun range.

Random dude walks into the bathroom, gets shocked look on face, and walks out. Clapper finishes taping the wire to Hubert's chest.

Hubert: A gun range. Really? All you're gonna hear are gunshots.

Clapper: Can't risk losing valuable intel, kid.

Another random dude walks in.

Hubert: I should get paid double for this.

Random dude gags and walks out.

Scene 3

Hubert is knocking on Sophia's door. The wire is itchy and he's noticeably scratching.

Sophia: Hey Hubert!

Hubert (scratching intensely): Hey Sophia.

Sophia: You ok?

Hubert: Oh, sure. I've just got a really bad rash.

Sophia (trying to not look disgusted): So what brings you by?

Hubert: Well, I thought I'd take you up on your offer to go to the gun range.

Sophia: Really? Great! Come on in!

Hubert happily strolls into Sophia's place. When they enter the living room, Hubert is shocked to see a strong, good looking guy sitting on the sofa.

Guy on Sofa: Hey dude! I'm Tom.

Hubert (gulps): Hey Tom. I'm Hubert.

Sophia: Tom, Hubert's gonna come to the range with us! Fresh meat, too. He's a rookie!

Tom: Really? Cool Are ya nervous?

Hubert: Um, no. Why would I be nervous?

Tom: No reason. The first time I went to the range, I got shot in the kneecap, but ya know, it happens.

Hubert (freaking out): What!?

Tom (laughing): Just kiddin, bro. Take it easy.

Sophia: Tom, you're terrible. I just gotta grab something from my room, then I'll be all set.

Sophia exits. Hubert notices a book in Tom's hand.

Hubert: May I ask what you're reading?

Tom: "The Most Dangerous Superstition" by Larken Rose. Have you read it?

Hubert: Nope. I haven't read a book since high school.

Tom: I'm not sure I'd readily admit that to people. Anyway, I'm borrowing it from Sophia.

Sophia enters.

Sophia: Awesome book! You're gonna love it, Tom.

Tom: How does it compare to Rothbard?

Sophia: Well, Rothbard is more about the economics of liberty. Larken hits more on the logic and morality of anarchy.

Hubert (confused face): Economics of liberty? You mean like capitalism and socialism?

Sophia (rolling eyes, giggling): Not exactly. Come on, let's go.

Scene 4

At an indoor shooting range called "The Big Bang", Sophia, Hubert, and Tom are signing in. Hubert notices a sign that says "CASH ONLY".

Hubert: Cash only. That's not smart. What if someone robs the place?

Old, crusty cashier gives a sideways glance to Hubert.

Sophia (chuckling): Hubert, everyone here is armed. Only someone with an extremely violent death wish would ever dream of trying to rob this place.

Cashier hands Hubert a thick stack of papers.

Hubert: What's this?

Old Crusty Cashier: Basically, it's a legal waiver that says we're not responsible for anything that happens to you.

Hubert signs, the three put on goggles and ear protection, and enter the range. Upon entering, the loud, unmistakable pops of gunfire startle Hubert. He jumps, trips on some empty bullet casings, falls into the corner of a table where he hits his head, and then finally hits the floor, unconscious.

Sophia (screaming): Oh my God! Hubert!

End Episode 6

Episode 7

Scene 1

Hubert is waking up in a hospital bed. Sophia is by his side.

Hubert (groggy, looking up at Sophia): Whoa.

Sophia: Something like that. How ya feeling?

Hubert: Drowsy, a painful headache, with a sprinkle of embarrassment and a dash of shame.

Sophia: Oh, don't be. It could happen to anyone.

Hubert starts reaching for his face.

Sophia: Don't touch your face.

Hubert: Why not?

Sophia: Stitches.

A male nurse and female doctor enter the room.

Doctor: Hey, you're awake! That's great! Do you remember what happened?

Hubert: Yeah, I guess. I fell, hit my head, and wound up here.

Doctor: Good enough. No signs of memory loss. We should be able to have you out of here within the hour.

Hubert: Wow, that fast?

Doctor: Yep, ER is filling up fast, and we need the space.

Hubert (sarcastic); How touching.

Doctor: Hubert, I see that you're behind on your shots. We'll go ahead and give you a flu shot, Hep B, and Hep C, ok? After that, you can go home.

Sophia: I wouldn't do it if I were you, Hubert. You don't have to.

Doctor: Sure, he can get sick if he wants.

Sophia: I never get any shots and I haven't been sick in years. Hubert, do you know the ingredients in the vaccines they want to give you?

Hubert shrugs.

Sophia: For that matter, do you know the ingredients, doctor?

Doctor: I'm just doing my job. (turns to exit) Nurse, I'll let you handle it from here.

Nurse: I'll tell ya what, man. The flu is especially nasty this year. I'd at least get that one. You know how many trillions of pathogens are floating around this hospital as we speak?

Sophia (arms crossed): Nice scare tactic.

Hubert: Ok, I'll take it. Just the flu shot, though.

Nurse prepares shot, then jabs into Hubert's arm.

Nurse: See, nothing to it! (pulls lolly-pop out of pocket) That's for you, for being a good boy. Ok, I'll go get the paperwork and your stuff so you can go home.

Hubert: Stuff?
Nurse: Yeah, ya know, possessions.

Hubert thinks to himself about the wire he was wearing....

Hubert: Oh, right. Yeah, ya know, I don't really need my stuff.
You can just toss it.

Nurse (confused): I'm not gonna do that, but you can do it later
after the drugs wear off, ok?

Nurse leaves.

Sophia: I'll wait and give you a ride.

30 minutes later....Nurse enters with plastic bag marked
"personal items" and a mountain of paperwork.

Hubert (anxious): Um, Sophia, I could really use something from
the cafeteria. I'm starved.

Sophia: We can stop on the way home and get something that's
not GMO crap if ya want.

Hubert: I'm just super hungry and don't know if I can wait.

Sophia: Ok, I'll be back.

Sophia leaves. Nurse hands Hubert his stuff.

Nurse: She's way too good looking to be your girlfriend or a
blood relative, so what gives?

Hubert: Thanks.

Nurse: And I don't like to pry, but what's this wire thingy in your stuff. I would think that you were some kind of secret agent if you weren't so, well, ya know.

Hubert: What's that supposed to mean?

Nurse: You don't exactly have a James Bond physique.

Hubert: Right, well, it's just a stupid cyborg club I'm in, that's all.

Nurse: That does sound pretty stupid. Well, just sign like a million times throughout this thick book of legalese and you'll be free.

Nurse leaves. Hubert hurriedly gets up and throws wire in the bathroom trash.

Scene 2

The next day at Nerd Squad headquarters in Fried Electronics store, Billy and Melinda are sitting around doing nothing, zoned out on their phones.

Billy: So I'm having a poker game at my place tonight.

Melinda: I don't believe you.

Billy: Why not?

Melinda: Because I know you don't have friends.

Billy (huffy): Ok, so it's an online poker game.

Melinda: With people you've never met.

Billy: Right.

Melinda: And people you'll never meet.

Billy: You should come serve me drinks.

Hubert enters. Billy and Melinda immediately notice the large gash with stitches on Hubert's forehead.

Billy: Whoa! Did she actually try to kill you?

Hubert (embarrassed): No, she didn't.

Melinda: What happened?

Hubert: I'd rather not talk about it.

Billy: You sound stuffed up.

Hubert (sniffling): Yeah, I think I'm getting sick.

Billy and Melinda back away with repulsed looks. Melinda grabs bottle of Lysol and aims it at Hubert.

Melinda (yelling): Berry, Hubert's sick! Get him out of here!

Berry pokes head out from office.

Berry (yelling): How about I send you home instead!

Melinda: That makes zero sense, but I'll take it!

Berry: You're not leaving, either! We've got a lot of service calls this afternoon! Hey, Hubert, how'd it go spying on your anarchist neighbor last night?!

Hubert (peering around with grimace on face): I don't know what you're talking about! Stop yelling!

Hubert's FBI handler, Richard Clapper, walks in.

Hubert (talking to self): My life just keeps getting better.

Clapper: Hubert, why haven't you been answering your phone? And why did your feed die last night? The last thing I heard was ker-plunk!

Hubert: It's a long story. Are you sure you should talk about this in front of other people?

Clapper: Are you sick? You sound weaker than normal.

Hubert: Thanks. Yeah, I got a flu shot at the hospital and I think it made me sick. Sophia tried to warn me against it, but.

Clapper cuts him off

Clapper: Oh, so she's one of those anti-vaxxers, huh? (shaking head disapprovingly) This girl is worse than I expected! We're looking at a real deep conspiracy here, real deep. Anyway, where's the wire?

Hubert: I threw it away.

Clapper (frantic): Why'd you do that?!

Hubert: Cuz Sophia gave me a ride home, and I didn't want her to see it. What's the big deal?

Clapper: It says "property of FBI" on it, that's why!

Hubert: That's not very clandestine.

Billy: What century are you guys in? Why wear a ridiculous wire when you have a smartphone?

Clapper: Hmmm, I didn't think of that.

Melinda: You're not the brightest bulb on the federal tree, are ya?

Billy: Clapper, you play poker?

Scene 3

That night, Hubert is laying in bed sick when his phone starts to ring.

Hubert: Please don't be Clapper. Hello?

Sophia: Hey Hubert. Just wanted to check up on ya.

Hubert: I'm sick.

Sophia: Sorry to hear that. I tried to warn you about that flu shot.

Hubert: Yeah, thanks for reminding me.

Sophia: I've got some natural medicine I can bring over if you want.

Hubert: Well, I've got Nylenol and TyQuil, so I think I'll manage.

Sophia: What I've got will actually work, and a lot faster. Wanna give it a try?

Hubert: Sure, come on over.

5 minutes later, Sophia comes into Hubert's place.
Sophia: Wow, you look like crap!

Hubert cringes.

Sophia: So I brought some bio-active silver hydrosol, some peppermint and eucalyptus oil, and some Manuka honey.

Hubert: Sounds delicious.

Sophia: It's a hell of a lot tastier than those chemical cocktails you've been taking.

Scene 4

2 days later, Hubert is calling Sophia

Hubert: I'm a hundred percent better!

Sophia: Stuff works fast, huh?

Hubert: Yeah, where'd you learn about natural medicine?

Sophia: I read stuff online, but I also have a friend who's a naturopathic doctor. You should meet her!

Hubert: Sure, maybe we can all go to the gun range together.

Sophia (cringing): Yeah.....or a different place. I'll call ya later, ok?

Call ends. Hubert's phone rings again.

Hubert: Hey Clapper.

Clapper: Hey, heard you've got another meeting lined up with Sophia. And with one of those quack doctors! That's great! More intel for us, and more money for you!

Hubert: How do you know all this?

Clapper: We decided to actively listen to your calls.

Hubert: You what?!

Clapper: Part of the deal, son, part of the deal. Don't meet up with them until I give you further instructions.

Scene 5

Clapper is having a meeting with his boss, Mr. Prick, at FBI headquarters.

Mr. Prick: Dammit, Clapper! Do you know what this means?!

Clapper (on edge of seat): Tell me, sir.

Mr. Prick: This could be an anarcho-nature-o-doctor conspiracy! You could be blowing the lid off of a major terrorist group!

Clapper: This is very exciting, sir.

Mr. Prick: Damn right it's exciting! You continue to justify our jobs! Now Clapper, here's what I need you to do. That little nerd you've been handling so far, what's his name, Pubert?

Clapper: Hubert, sir.

Mr. Prick: Right. This is getting serious and I can't let him go it alone anymore. You're going to have to join him on his next mission. Is that clear?

Clapper: Are you sure that's a good idea sir?

Mr. Prick: Of course it's a good idea! I thought of it, didn't I?

Clapper: Of course, sir. I'll notify Hubert right away.

End Episode 7

Episode 8

Scene 1

At Nerd Squad headquarters in Fried Electronics store, Melinda
and Billy are tossing pennies at unsuspecting customers' feet in
order to see who's cheap enough to pick them up. Hubert is
watching.

Billy: Check out this ancient guy over there. Guaranteed he
picks this up. People from the Great Depression era still think
pennies have value.

Melinda: Maybe, but I don't think his back can take it. He
doesn't look too spry.

Billy: Wanna put a wager on that?

Melinda: Nah, I don't want to contribute to your voracious
gambling habit.

Billy: How about you, Hubert?

Hubert: Sure. If I win, I get to slam your head in the wall. If you
win, you get to slam your head in the wall.

Billy (rubbing head): I'm not falling for that one again.

Billy pitches the penny at the old man's feet. The old man tries to
pick it up, then grimaces in pain, grabs his back, curses, and
walks off.

Melinda: Told ya!

Billy: Hubert, what's your problem today? You're acting a lot
weirder and psycho than normal.

Hubert (huffy): OH, I'm just stressed over my next encounter with Sophia.

Melinda: Encounter? What happened? She turn into an alien or something?

Hubert: No, it's just that Clapper insisted that he come to meet her. How am I going to justify bringing that freak with me?

Billy: Just tell her that Clapper is your dad.

Melinda: I'd believe that.

Billy: Or you could just tell her the truth, that your FBI boss wants to spy on her with you.

Hubert: You guys are a huge help.

Berry (yelling from his office): Hey, what are you guys talking about?!

Billy: We're plotting a mutiny against you!

Berry: Cool, then I can collect unemployment!

Melinda: You mean unenjoyment?!

Billy: So what's the date with Sophia?

Hubert: She's having a meetup at her place. People from some social media website focused on freelancing.

Hubert's phone starts ringing. He looks at the number and frowns.

Hubert: Hey Clapper.

Clapper: Hey, so here's the deal. You're gonna introduce me to Sophia as your uncle.

Hubert: Please don't make her think we're related.

Clapper: It's a done deal, son. It was my boss' stupid idea. I'm not too thrilled about it either. You're not the sharpest tack on the bulletin board, ya know.

Hubert: Be there at seven.

Click.

Hubert dials Sophia

Hubert: Hey Sophia, it's Hubert. I hate to do this, but my uncle is in town and I'd feel really guilty just leaving him home alone. You mind if he comes?

Sophia: The more the merrier!

Hubert: I hope you still feel that way after you meet him.

Sophia: What?

Hubert: Nothing. See ya tonight.

Click.

Billy: Hubert, I'm impressed. You've become quite proficient at lying.

Hubert: I guess the FBI is rubbing off on me.

Scene 2

Hubert is meeting Richard Clapper in the parking lot of Hubert's apartment complex.

Clapper: Ok, Hubert, this is the first time we've gone on a top secret mission together.

Hubert: It's just a meetup at a friend's house, not a mission.
Clapper (flabbergasted): What?! We're about to walk into the core of an anarchist conspiracy! The world is counting on us. They're not your friends, Hubert.

Hubert: Your delusions of grandeur are truly frightening.

Clapper: Whatever, you'll see. So anyway, if anything goes haywire and I need to give you a warning signal, I'll give you a codeword.

Hubert rolls eyes and sighs deeply.

Clapper: The codeword is "Hoover".

Hubert (stunned, in a mocking sense): Hoover?

Clapper: Yeah, ya know, like J. Edgar.

Hubert: So you're just gonna blurt out "Hoover" if you think something has gone awry?! Gee, that's not suspicious at all.

Clapper: You got a better idea?

Hubert: Yeah! Go home, and let me enjoy this party!

Clapper: Not a chance, kid. This could be my big break. Come on, let's roll.

They walk up to Sophia's door and Hubert knocks.

Sophia: Hi Hubert! This must be your uncle.

Hubert: Yep, he must be.

Clapper: Hi, I'm Richard Clapper. Aren't you a pretty little thang? You can call me Dick.

Hubert: Or Captain Inappropriate, like everyone else in our family calls him.

Sophia (awkward face): Maybe just Rich. Come on in!

They walk in and there are around 20 people chatting in various areas of the apartment.

Sophia: There are so many cool people here! I'm glad you came. So I'm drinking tequila. You guys interested?

Hubert: Oh, I don't drink, really.

Clapper: Come on Hubert, don't be such a pansy!

Hubert: Ok, tequila it is!

Sophia leads them into the kitchen, grabs a bottle, and pours shots. They all down the shots, followed by a severe coughing fit by Hubert.

Clapper (slapping Hubert on the back): Told ya he's a pansy!

Sophia cringes, then spots her friend Zee.

Sophia: Hi Zee! I want you to meet Hubert.

Zee: Hi Hubert!

Clapper: And I'm Richard Clapper, Hubert's handsome, sophisticated, and wealthy uncle.

Hubert: And you forgot delusional.

Zee gives a concerned smile.

Zee: So, are you guys freelancers, too?

Hubert: Not exactly.

Zee: Oh, I just assumed you were. Sorry.

Clapper (suspicious voice): Why did you assume that?

Zee: Because this is a meetup for freelancers.

Clapper grunts.

Sophia: Zee, you blog mostly about crypto, right?

Zee: Well, I...

Clapper cuts her off

Clapper: You mean like Tales From The Crypt?

Zee (uncomfortable laugh): You're funny.

Hubert (shameful face): No, he's not.

Zee: I also write a lot of fiction with morality and anarchy themes.

Sophia: Cool, the world could use more of that, for sure.

Hubert: You actually make money writing on there?

Sophia: Yep! My photography does pretty well, too. You should try it!

Hubert: Well, my dead end job would be pretty hard to give up, but maybe I could give it a shot.

Zee: So Richard, what do you do?

Clapper: I work for the FBI.

Hubert's eyes bulge and his mouth drops open. All the nearby chatter stops and you can just about hear a pin drop.

Sophia: Are you serious?

Clapper (proud, pats himself on belly): Yep, almost twenty years.

Sophia: I'm sorry, but I have to ask you to leave.

Clapper: What?

Hubert: Really?

Sophia: Yeah, I'm sorry Hubert, I know he's your family and all, but I can't associate with people like that.

Clapper (offended, hands on hips): People like what?

Sophia: Long story short, criminals.

Clapper: How do ya figure that!?

Sophia: Because you're funded by a form of extortion called taxation.

Clapper: Well, ya can't just kick me out.

Hubert: Actually, it's her apartment, so she can.

Clapper: Ok, I see how it is. (starts walking away. Hubert doesn't follow) Well, Hubert, come on!

Hubert: I kinda wanna stay here.

Clapper: Hubert!

Sophia: It's ok, Hubert. Go with him. See ya later, ok?

Chatter resumes as they make their way out.

Scene 3

Clapper is having a meeting with his boss, Mr. Prick, at Prick's office.

Prick: Dammit, Clapper! (slams fist on desk) Ya told her your real name?

Clapper: Yes, sir.

Prick: And ya told her that you worked for the FBI?

Clapper: Yeah, so?

Prick (slams fist on desk again): Dammit, Clapper! What the hell do ya think "top secret" means?

Clapper: Well, I didn't tell her I was there to spy on her.

Prick: Ok, Clapper, listen up. This is how it's gonna be. You're not to ever get personally involved in this case again!

Clapper: It was your idea to send me with Hubert, sir.

Prick: Dammit, Clapper! I know that! So this girl kicked you out just cuz you're FBI?

Clapper: Yes, sir.

Prick: Dammit, Clapper! Why didn't you shoot her?

Clapper: It must've been the tequila, sir. I wasn't thinking straight.

Prick: That much is certain, Clapper. Dammit! (huffs) You said there were 20 people at this little gathering?

Clapper: Yes, sir.

Prick: Then this is far too big for little Hubert to handle. And you've proven yourself worse than Hubert. So here's what you're gonna do. I want you to recruit another one of those nerds from Hubert's store for this case. I want Sophia's known and unknown associations mapped out!

Clapper: Unknown associations, sir?

Prick: Dammit, Clapper! What part of unknown associations do you not understand?!

Clapper: Sorry, sir. Mapping unknown associations makes perfect sense.

Prick: Damn right it does! Now get the hell out of my face, Clapper! Your country, and my promotion, are counting on you!

Clapper: Yes, sir!
End Episode 8

Episode 9

Scene 1

At Nerd Squad headquarters in Fried Electronics store, Billy and Melinda are working intensely on a laptop. Their boss, Berry, walks in.

Berry: Why are you two being so diligent?

Melinda (looking up from computer): Berry, you decided to crawl out of your boss man cave? What's the occasion?

Berry: I'm going to have a drink at Happy's across the street.

Billy (looks up from screen): Is it 11am already?

FBI agent Richard Clapper walks in.

Clapper: Hey, is Hubert around?

Berry: No, I fired him.

Clapper: I don't blame ya.

Berry: Just kiddin, he'll be here in a bit.

Clapper: Billy, Melinda, what are you two up to?

Melinda: We're hacking the FBI.

Clapper: Funny girl, funny girl. Seriously, I've never seen you two actually work, so what's going on?

Billy: If you must know, we hacked Hubert's phone and now we're in the process of signing him up for Tinder and messaging as many people on there as possible.

Clapper: You can do that?

Berry: Yeah, you can do that?

Melinda (slaps Billy on shoulder): Cat's out of the bag now! Now he's gonna expect quality work from both of us.

Clapper (turns to Berry): I need to talk to your employees privately. Would you mind?

Berry: Not at all, I was on my way out to do some good deeds anyway.

Clapper: You're a horrible liar.

Berry leaves.

Clapper: So I've got great news. We're expanding the program. I'll need one of you to help Hubert on his mission.

Billy: You mean hang out with him and his dream girl slash anarchist neighbor?

Clapper: Yep! Considering both of you work here, I know you could use the extra cash!

Billy and Melinda nod sadly.

Clapper: So here's the deal. You two are gonna have a competition for the job. I want both of you to spy on Hubert. Whoever gets the most valuable intel in the next 48 hours gets the job. How about it?

Melinda: You do realize that spying on Hubert is kind of like spying on the drying of paint.

Billy: Not now that he has this Tinder account.

Clapper: So it's a deal?

Billy and Melinda both agree. Hubert walks in. Billy and Melinda slam the laptop shut.

Hubert: Hey Clapper, what are you doing here?

Clapper: Just checking up on ya. Well, gotta run!

Hubert: I just got here.

Clapper: Yep, and ya look normal, so that's great.

Clapper runs away.

Hubert: That was weird.

Billy: Clapper's always weird.

Hubert: True.

Scene 2

Clapper is waiting in the Fried Electronics parking lot. When Billy comes out, he approaches in an awkward, paranoid way.

Billy: Hey Clapper.

Clapper (whispering): Try to keep your voice down.

Billy: What kind of drugs did you take?

Clapper: Just what my psychiatrist gave me. Why do you ask?

Billy cringes.

Clapper: Anyway, I gotta tell ya something. Your mission isn't really to spy on Hubert. That was just a cover. I really want you to spy on Melinda.

Billy: Sounds creepy. (pause) I'll do it. How much ya gonna pay me?

Clapper: You don't get paid for a tryout, son.

Billy (exhaling deeply and looking to the heavens): Thank god I'm not your son. So what about Melinda?

Clapper (awkwardly searching for a good lie): Oh, um, I don't think she'll cut it. But I still need you to prove yourself.

Billy: Ok, cool. I gotta go. I'm on a service call.

Billy gets in his car and leaves.

A few minutes later, Melinda comes out.

Clapper: Psst!

Melinda tries to ignore him.

Clapper (stealthy): Hey.

Melinda: Clapper, can't you tell when someone is ignoring you?

Clapper: You knew I was here?

Melinda: I saw you as soon as I came out of the building.

Clapper (embarrassed): Oh, well then. Ok, anyway, I've got to talk with ya. Ya know that whole spying on Hubert thing?

Melinda: Yeah?

Clapper: Not gonna happen.

Melinda: Why not?

Clapper: Your real mission is to spy on Billy.

Melinda: Billy? The creepy Billy I work with?

Clapper: Yeah.

Melinda: That's really gross and boring. I'm not sure I'm up for it.

Clapper: Oh, come on, he seems like a decent fella.

Melinda: That's not saying much, coming from you.

Clapper: Well, look, that's the deal. Take it or leave it.

Melinda (sighs, rolls eyes): Oh, all right.

Clapper: Great! You'll hear from me in 48 hours!

Scene 3

Later in the day, Billy and Melinda are heading to their cars at the end of their shift.

Billy: So, where ya headed?

Melinda: Home, of course.

Billy: You live in city heights, right?

Melinda (blushing): Nope.

Billy (narrows eyes): Really?

Melinda: Where are you headed?

Billy: You know I have no life.

Melinda: True. We should maybe go grab a drink, so we can get to know each other better.

Billy (throws hands up): Ok, now I know something isn't right. You're asking me to go out with you?

Melinda: Why is that weird?

Billy: Cuz you're hot and you know I'm desperate. This doesn't add up. Wait a minute...…Did you see Clapper when you went on that service call today?

Melinda: Um, maybe. Why? Did you?

Billy: Yes, I did. Damn that Clapper.

Melinda: What are you thinking?

Billy: He asked me to spy on you.

Melinda: He asked me to spy on you!

Billy (pumped up): Oh, it's on now!

Melinda: Dare I ask what that hamster wheel in your head is turning out?

Billy: We're gonna give Clapper a dose of his own medicine.

Scene 4

Hubert is knocking on Sophia's door.

Sophia: Hey Hubert!

Hubert: Hey, it's been a while.

Sophia: Yeah, since the meetup.

Hubert: You're not mad about that, are you?

Sophia (sarcastic): No, why would I be mad that you brought an FBI order-follower to my house?

Hubert (cringing): Yeah, sorry about that.

Sophia: No worries. Wanna come in?

Hubert: Of course.

Sophia: I'm in the middle of planning a big event.

Hubert: Is that right? What, like a party?

Sophia: Nope, even better! A TSA walk through! It's gonna be epic!

Hubert: I don't get it.

Sophia: I've been raising funds to buy some cheap air tickets. I can hopefully get at least 50 people to join me. The plan is to walk through a TSA checkpoint and refuse all searches. No radiation, no touching, nothing. Just walk on through like it should be for a free individual.

Hubert (mousy): Sounds kinda risky.

Sophia: Yeah, freedom doesn't come easy in this world, that's for sure. You wanna come?

Hubert: Won't we get arrested?

Sophia: I don't think they could arrest all of us. That's why I want at least 50 people. And who knows, some of us might actually get to fly, too. (persuasive voice) Come on, free flight! Will ya do it?

Hubert: How many people do you have so far?

Sophia: Three.

Hubert: So I won't hold my breath, then.

Scene 5

The next day at Nerd Squad headquarters.....

Melinda: So Hubert, when will you see Clapper again?

Hubert (disturbed look): Why do you care?

Melinda: I just wanted to talk with him, that's all.

Berry (yelling from his office chair): What!?

Hubert: Yeah, what?

Melinda: I just think he's kinda interesting, that's all.

Berry (shouting): What does he have that I don't have?!

Billy: That's a good point. They're both old, bald, and creepy.

Berry: Look who's talking!

Billy: No, I'm young, balding, and creepy! Big difference!

Melinda: So can I get his number?

Berry: Damn twilight zone all to hell!

Hubert: Well, I dunno. Sure, why not? I don't care if he fires me anyway.

Billy: Ya don't? You're making triple what you make here.

Berry: Yeah, why do you still work here, Hubert!? You should quit!

Hubert: Yeah, but every day I feel more and more guilty about the situation with Sophia.

Billy: Don't worry, Hubert. She'll stop hanging out with you eventually, anyway. FBI or not.

Hubert cringes.

Hubert: Anyway, sure, I'll text you his number right now.

Later that afternoon, Melinda is calling Clapper.

Clapper: Romeo Valerio speaking.

Melinda: What?!

Clapper: Who's this?

Melinda: Hey Clap-man, it's Melinda. Who's Romeo Valerio?

Clapper: Top secret. How'd you get my number?

Melinda (sexy voice): So I'm heading out to drink and be irresponsible. Wanna come?

Clapper (shocked and joyful): Um, uh, ya, ya, I'll do that.

Melinda: Great! I'll text you the address. Bye.

Click.

Billy: Game on?

Melinda (smirking): Game on.

End Episode 9

Episode 10

Scene 1

Melinda and Billy are having a chat before they set out to spy on FBI agent Richard Clapper.

Melinda: So I'm meeting Clapper at The Trendy Bar.

Billy: Perfect. That's a good place to blend in with all the other fake people.

Melinda (offended): Hey!

Billy: And what am I gonna do?

Melinda: Wait in your car. When I'm done with him, you'll follow him home.

Billy: Why do I have to be the one to go to that creep's house?

Melinda: Because he's falling head over heels to drink with me, not you. Besides, you get the better end of the deal as far as I'm concerned. What if he tries to touch me?

Billy: Good point.

Scene 2

Hubert is at Sophia's place.

Sophia: Wanna go to The Trendy Bar?

Hubert: Um, isn't that the place where totally superficial people who are full of themselves hang out?

Sophia: Yep, that about sums it up.

Hubert: Doesn't exactly seem like your kinda spot.

Sophia: It's not. I just go there to plant seeds.

Hubert: Ok, ya totally lost me.

Sophia: I plant seeds of liberty by using what you might call "choice commentary". Come on, it'll be fun!

Scene 3

Melinda walks into The Trendy Bar. The place has plenty of trendies chatting and texting away, while bad pop music plays in the background. Clapper is seated at a booth facing the front entrance. Upon seeing Melinda enter, he gets a huge cheesy grin and starts waving his arms frantically.

Clapper: Hey, over here! I'm over here!

Melinda (cringing fake smile): Hi!

She takes a seat and Clapper leans in real close to her face, which causes her to instantly pull away in disgust.

Clapper: Man, this place is hip!

Melinda: What's wrong with your hip?

Clapper: No, no, this place! It's hip!

Melinda (confused): I don't know what that means.

Clapper: What? Ya know, hip, like groovy, cool, far out.

Melinda: Oh, I get it, it's an old expression. Old man, old lingo. Got it.

Clapper: I'm not that old.

Melinda: You actually are, compared to me, but that's ok. I like older guys.

Clapper: Ya do? Wow. (starts fawning face)

A waiter shows up to take their order.

Waiter: Drinks?

Clapper: Appletini,, make it a double.

Waiter cringes.

Melinda (to Clapper): So you're buying, right?

Clapper: Uh, well ..

Melinda: Sounds like a yes to me. (turns to waiter) I'll also have a shot of whatever your top shelf tequila is.

Waiter: Is he your dad?

Melinda: No.

Waiter: Relative?

Melinda: Definitely not related.

Waiter: Why are you with him? I'm confused.

Clapper: Lay off, buddy. I'm FBI.

Waiter: Oh, now I get it. (walks away)

Clapper: What the hell did he mean by that?

Melinda: Are you sure you should tell people so openly about being FBI?

Clapper: Probably not, but once in a while I like to show off.

Hubert and Sophia walk into the bar. Sophia spots Clapper.

Sophia: Hey, isn't that your uncle?

Hubert looks and shudders at the sight.

Hubert: Yeah, how unbelievably unfortunate.

Sophia: Are you gonna say hi?

Hubert: Absolutely not. Come on, let's go sit on the far end of the bar so we don't get spotted.

Sophia; Real loving family.

Hubert and Sophia take a couple spots at the bar. The bartender approaches.

Sophia: How many violence-backed federal reserve notes is a shot of top shelf tequila?

Bartender (confused): Um, what? Top shelf shot is 50 bucks.

Sophia: Got it. 50 violence-backed federal reserve notes. 2 shots, please.

Hubert (eyeing Clapper and Melinda): Why the hell is she with him?

Sophia: Who?

Hubert: That girl that's with Clapper, I mean, Uncle Clapper. She's my co-worker.

Sophia: Bizarre.

Meanwhile, at Clapper's table…..

Melinda (takes deep breath): Ok, so anyway, I'm really anxious to get to know you, Clapper.

Clapper: You are?

Melinda: Yep.

Clapper: Well, what do ya wanna know?

Melinda: When's your birthday?

Clapper: April first.

Melinda: How fitting. And how old are you?

Clapper: Fifty-nine. And you?

Melinda: A lot younger. I'm really curious about your mother's maiden name.

Clapper: Clapper.

Melinda: But, isn't that your father's name? That's why you go by Clapper?

Clapper: Well, both my parents had the last name Clapper. Real tight knit family.

Melinda (shocked): TMI. Ok, moving on.

Waiter drops off drinks. Melinda slams her shot.

Melinda (to waiter): Keep 'em coming! (to Clapper) Ok, so where were we? Where were you born?

Clapper: A little town in South Florida called Homestead.

Melinda: What's the name of the street you grew up on?

Clapper: Clapper Drive.

Melinda: Come on, no way.

Clapper: Yep, small town. We got to name the street.

Melinda: Do you have a lucky number?

Clapper: 9,350.

Melinda (narrows eyes): Wow, quite the number. Hey, I just realized, I don't have your email.

Clapper: RichardClapper69 at hotmailer dot com.

Melinda (shouting): Waiter! Where's that damn shot?!

Melinda: With all that big money you make, I bet you need more than one bank account.

Clapper: Nah, just the one down at Hells Largo.

Waiter brings another shot. Melinda slams it.

Melinda: Well, Clapper, thanks for the drinks! I gotta run.

Clapper: Already? Can I give ya a lift?

Melinda: No, thanks. I'll find any other way to get home.

Melinda leaves. Shortly after, Clapper leaves as well. Billy follows him to his house.

Billy (talking to himself while noting the house number): Man, what a dump. He sold his soul and this is all he gets? Sick world we live in.

Scene 3

The next day at Nerd Squad headquarters in Fried Electronics store, Billy and Melinda are hacking away on two laptops getting into Clapper's data.

Berry (yelling from his private office): Hey, what are you hacking now?!

Melinda (gives disdainful look): I don't know what you're talking about!

Hubert walks in.

Hubert: Hey guys.

Billy: Welcome to work.

Hubert: So, Melinda, would you mind telling me what the hell you were doing at The Trendy Bar last night with Clapper?

Melinda: Don't know what you're talking about.

Hubert: I saw you, and so did Sophia.

Melinda: You must've been hallucinating.

Hubert (smug, arms crossed): So I guess if I talk to Clapper about it, then he'll deny it, too?

Melinda: Oh, fine. Don't tell Clapper, ok?

Berry (yelling): You've got leverage, Hubert! Use it!

Hubert takes a look at the laptop screen that Melinda is working on.

Hubert: What the? Are you hacking Clapper? Is that his bank account?

Billy: If you want to be technical, we're auditioning for a job with the FBI.

Hubert: What?

Billy: Clapper made a recruiting call here yesterday. He's giving us a tryout.

Hubert: Clapper put you up to this? He assigned you to hack him?

Melinda: Well, not exactly. But the way we see it, even if he doesn't hire us, this is way too much fun messing with a scumbag like that.

Berry (shouting): Hey, you guys hacked Clapper's bank account?!

A casually browsing customer hears this and gets an offended look on face, then runs away.

Melinda (angry): Berry! What did we say about shouting stuff like that!

Berry: I was just gonna say you should buy us all lunch! Or, he should, rather!

Hubert: You aren't going to actually take money, are you?

Melinda: No, we just wanna see what he has, and that's it.

Billy starts cackling.

Hubert: What? What's so funny?

Billy: Ok, maybe that's not entirely it. I was thinking about what else we did.

Hubert: Like what?

Billy: Subscribed him to some highly specialized adult sites.

Hubert: Ok, I know too much. I'm walking away now.

Later that day, Clapper is talking with Billy.

Clapper: Ok, Billy, lay it on me. What did ya get on Melinda?

Billy: Nada.

Clapper: I don't get it.

Billy: It means nothing, in Spanish.

Clapper: Oh.

Billy: I'm sure you'll be impressed with what I did get. You, Richard Clapper, have enough money in your Hells Largo account to buy a modest used car. You were born in Homestead, Florida. You are subscribed to some highly questionable websites.

Clapper interrupts.

Clapper: Hey, hold on. You spied on me?

Billy: We. Meaning Melinda and I.

Clapper (flabbergasted): Well, I dunno what to say!
Billy gives bemused, smug look, and folds arms.

Clapper: I'm gonna have to hire both of you!

Billy (flabbergasted): Really?

Clapper: You, my friend, have what it takes. FBI material if I've ever seen it!

Billy: By stabbing you in the back, basically?

Clapper: Welcome to my world, kid.

Scene 4

Clapper is having a meeting at the office of his boss, Mr. Prick.

Mr. Prick (slams fist on desk): Dammit, Clapper! They got into your bank account!?

Clapper: Yes, sir. They're quite deceptive and clever.

Mr. Prick: Well, it doesn't take much to outwit you, Clapper, but it's impressive nonetheless!

Clapper: Thank you, sir.

Mr. Prick: That settles it then! I want both of them to help Hubert spy on that peace-loving anarchist, Sophia!

Clapper: Yes, sir. Damn those peace-lovers!

Mr. Prick (slams fist on desk): Dammit, Clapper, that's right! If the world has too many people like that, then we'll be out of a job and a pension!

Clapper: How terrifying to imagine!

Mr. Prick: Damn right it is, Clapper!

End Episode 10

Episode 11

Scene 1

Hubert, Melinda, and Billy are sitting around doing nothing at
Nerd Squad headquarters in Fried Electronics store.

Billy: So Hubert, we need to figure out how all three of us can
spy on Sophia without her getting suspicious.

Hubert (sighs): Or you two can just leave us alone and go get
your own, um, victim.

Melinda: Interesting choice of words.

Billy: How about a party? Yeah, a party at Hubert's place. You
invite Sophia, and Melinda and I will get introduced there.

Hubert: Bad idea.

Melinda: Why?

Hubert: Because I don't want you interfering in my relationship
with Sophia!

Billy (chuckles): Hubert, even if something did happen between
you two, how far can it really go? You think that at some point
she won't find out you've been spying on her for the FBI?

Berry (yelling from his office): Hey Billy, got a minute?!

Billy: No!

Berry: I just need to know what the problem with Mrs. Needleston's computer was! You just wrote "Felix" on the paperwork!
Billy: Felix is her cat!

Berry: What?!

Billy: Could you please come out here and talk to us so we don't have to yell!?

Berry: But I'm the boss!

Billy: We took a vote and decided that you should come out here instead!

Berry (to himself): Dammit.

Berry walks out and joins the others.

Berry: So what's Felix mean?

Billy: That's Mrs. Needleston's cat. He destroyed another power cord.
Berry: Another?

Billy: Yep, third time, so I just wrote Felix.

Hubert, Billy, and Melinda all stare at Berry.

Berry: Can you guys do some work, please?

Melinda: No.

Berry: Why not? I could fire you, ya know.

Melinda: You could, but you won't, that's why we call your bluff. We know you're too lazy to try and hire new people.

Berry: Dammit.
Billy (to Hubert): Anyway, as I was saying, before we were so rudely interrupted. Sophia will find out that you've been spying on her, and then at the very least, ignore you. At worst, find some creative ways to physically maim you.

Hubert: She wouldn't do that.

Melinda: I would.

Hubert (defensive): You're not her!

Billy: Hey man, it's Clapper's orders, so we're doing this with or without your cooperation. So party on Saturday?

Hubert: No, Saturday's no good.

Melinda: Why not?

Hubert: That's the day of the....(hesitates)

Melinda: The what?

Billy: Come on, Hubert. Spill it!

Hubert: Well, Sophia's been organizing a TSA protest. Well, not a protest exactly, just kind of a, well, she calls it asserting natural rights, but I dunno what to call it.

Melinda: What are you gonna do exactly?

Hubert: She's got about 50 people with tickets to fly at roughly the same time, and we're going to walk through a TSA checkpoint without stopping.

Berry: Sounds dangerous to me!

Melinda: Berry, open toed shoes sound dangerous to you.

Billy: I hate to agree with Berry, but he's right this time. You're gonna get tazed or something, Hubert.

Melinda: I've got it! We'll film it for her. Tell her we'd like to come and document it.

Billy: That's actually a nice, safe middle ground. Melinda, you're such a clever pragmatist. We reap the rewards without the risk.

Melinda: I assume you've already told Clapper about this little protest.

Hubert (mousy, glances at floor): Um, yeah, of course.

Melinda: You're lying.

Hubert: What? No I'm not.

Melinda: One more lie and I'll tell Berry about that thing from Chicago.

Berry: Thing from Chicago?

Hubert: Low blow, Melinda, very low blow. (sighs) No, I haven't told Clapper. We can't! He'll send agents to stop it before it even starts. At least this way we have a chance of not getting beaten or thrown in jail.

Billy: Yeah, we'll decide whether or not to tell Clapper later.

Melinda: Oh, all right. (sticks finger in Hubert's face) We'd better get paid, though.

Scene 2

It's Saturday, and Hubert and Sophia are driving to the airport to meet up with the other volunteers for the TSA walk through.

Hubert (nervous): Um, remind me why we're doing this again?

Sophia: To assert our natural right to travel unobstructed.

Hubert: But the TSA doesn't stop people from traveling, do they?

Sophia: Not as long as you let them invade your privacy and radiate you and steal your water.

Hubert: Hmmm, I never looked at it like that. How did you pay for all those tickets, anyway?

Sophia: Some people bought their own tickets and the rest of the money was raised via donations. Tell your friends thanks for recording it, by the way.

Hubert: Friends might be a stretch.

They pull into an airport parking lot.
Sophia: Ok, we're here! You look nervous.

Hubert: Nah, I always sweat in air conditioned cars and have a pulse of 160.

Sophia: Ok, just 30 minutes. Let's go get our boarding passes and I'll text everyone to confirm.

They get out of the car and take a few steps.

Hubert: Wait, just a sec.

Hubert leans against a light post and vomits violently.

Hubert: Ok, I'm good.

Scene 3

Sophia and Hubert are immersed in a group of about 50 people near the terminal 1 TSA checkpoint. Sophia is communicating with the group via an encrypted chat app, so as not to draw attention to the group and what's about to happen. Billy and Melinda approach Sophia and Hubert.

Melinda: Almost showtime, huh?

Hubert looks around awkwardly, trying to ignore her.

Billy (overzealous smile): Hubert, you should introduce us.

Sophia: Wait! Don't tell me. You must be Billy and Melinda!

Melinda: Did you know that just because we're the only other people that talk to Hubert willingly?

Hubert (sarcastic): I'm so glad you guys are here.

Sophia (cringing): Ok, well, it's almost time to walk through the immoral security theater of the absurd. You guys ready to record?

Billy: Yep, sure thing. We'll be a very safe distance away, valiantly recording.

Melinda: And playing dumb if anyone asks if we know you.

Sophia sends out a message and within the next minute, a few rows of people start walking into the TSA checkpoint area. They don't stop to put their stuff through the scanners. They don't stop to get scanned. They don't respond to any of the ludicrous orders from the ignorant, uniformed order-followers. The order-followers don't know what to do. They're outnumbered 50 to 6. One gets on a radio and calls for the police to come. The entire group gets through unscathed and split into different directions towards different gates and different flights.

However, while Hubert is rounding a corner just past the checkpoint, he gets hit by an oncoming electric cart. Before he has a chance to recover, a TSA worker catches up and falls on him. A moment later, the police show up and taze Hubert.

Scene 4

Hubert is in an airport holding cell. Hubert is pacing around frantically, mumbling to himself. The door flings open.

Clapper: Hubert!

Hubert: Clapper? What are you doing here?

Clapper: Getting you out of trouble. (shuts door)

Hubert: You mean I'm not going to prison?

Clapper: Nope.

Hubert: My life isn't over?

111

Clapper: Your life was over long before we met. Anyway, congratulations on being the only one from that little protest to get caught! That really says something.

Hubert: Wait….You knew about it?

Clapper: Yeah, of course!
Hubert: But how?

Clapper: Your new partners from the Nerd Squad, Billy and Melinda. They also said that you didn't want to tell me.

Hubert (shuffling uncomfortably): No, I didn't…..say that, exactly.

Clapper: You guys are stabbing each other in the back already! I love it! Just goes to show you're real government material.

Hubert: It does?

Clapper: So anyway, I let the protest go ahead. I figure if your little anarchist friend, Sophia, gets away with a few things like that, then she'll try to do something bigger at some point. And that's when we strike!

Hubert: Strike?

Clapper: Hey, I know ya got tazed, and you look like hell, so go ahead and get out of here.

Scene 5

The next day, Clapper is meeting his FBI boss, Mr. Prick, in Mr. Prick's office.

Mr. Prick (slams fist on desk): Dammit, Clapper! What the hell were you thinking?!

Clapper (fumbling): Um, well, what do ya mean, sir?

Mr. Prick: You let those liberty lovers get away with thumbing their nose at the TSA! It's all over the internet!

Clapper: Well, yes, but if I could just explain my logic. Ya see...

Mr. Prick slams his fist on the desk and cuts him off....

Mr. Prick: Dammit, Clapper! No, you can't explain your logic! Ya know why?

Clapper: Well, sir, I....

Mr. Prick cuts him off again.

Mr. Prick: I wasn't really asking, dammit! Your logic is completely illogical, that's why! Don't you see? If they get a small victory like this, they'll consider even more brazen objectives! Worse yet, their message is spreading to others on the internet! Dammit, Clapper!

Clapper: It won't happen again, sir.

Mr. Prick: Now get out of here, Clapper!

Clapper: Yes, sir.

Mr. Prick: And get me a pastrami sandwich from Pauli's on the corner. That's your punishment for your undiligency.

Clapper (confused): Is undiligency a word, sir?

Mr. Prick: Dammit, Clapper! Hell if I know! Just go get that damned sandwich!

Clapper: Yes, sir.

Scene 6

Hubert walks into Fried Electronics and approaches Billy and Melinda. Billy starts applauding loudly.

Hubert: Ha, ha. Very funny.

Billy: Hubert, you're making me so much money on youtube right now, I might buy you a coffee or something.

Hubert (sighs): Ok, I'll bite. Why is that?

Billy shows a video playing on his phone. It's a video of Hubert getting blindsided by the electric cart.

Billy. Less than 24 hours, and already over 10,000 views!

Hubert: You recorded that?!

Melinda: Yeah, luckily there's a long glass-walled corridor right where you were walking when you got hit, so we had a chance to memorialize it forever!

Hubert (sarcastic): Great, just great. Oh, and thanks for telling Clapper about everything.

Melinda: Hey, you're lucky we did, or you might still be in that holding cell!

End Episode 11

Episode 12

Scene 1

Hubert and Sophia are sipping coffee at Sophia's place.

Hubert (sipping contentedly): Wow, I had no idea coffee could be this good.

Sophia: I know, right? Fresh and organic makes all the difference! 20 violence-backed federal reserve notes says you never drink Starmucks again!

Hubert: Not a bet I'll take. So I gotta ask, what's with all the random piles of plastic parts everywhere?

Sophia: I'm glad you asked. They're gun parts.

Hubert starts shaking involuntarily.

Hubert (nervous): Excuse me?

Sophia: I'm making a bunch of 3D printed guns.

Hubert (sarcastic): Is there a coup brewing that you haven't told me about?

Sophia (giggly): No, silly. Violence is wrong, remember? I'm going to a donation market this weekend. Guns are something I'm bringing to offer.

Hubert: I'm confused.

Sophia: So once a month, there's a huge kind of festival, free market, social event a couple hours from here, up in the mountains. It's pretty much anarchists that go there, but everyone is welcome, of course. And people trade via donations and gifts.

Hubert (uncertain): Not buying and selling.

Sophia: Well, let's say someone offers me a donation of crypto, and in return I offer a gift of one gun. We both voluntarily agree and make the trade. It's a beautiful way to circumvent extortion, well, taxation, as you call it.

Hubert: Hmmm, very clever.

Sophia: So you wanna go with me this weekend? It'll be a lot of fun, and you can help me assemble the guns.

Hubert (deep breath): Um, sure, I guess.

Sophia: Gee, Hubert, try to curb your enthusiasm.

Hubert: No, it's great, I'm just not comfortable in big groups.

Sophia: What do you call big?

Hubert: Any group bigger than, say, 2 people.

Sophia: Would you feel better with more familiar people around? Why don't you bring your friends from work, Melinda and Billy?

Hubert (grimacing): Oh, I dunno if that's such a good idea.

Sophia: Why not? The more the merrier!

Hubert: Famous last words.

Scene 2

Hubert, Melinda, and Billy are chatting at Nerd Squad headquarters at Fried Electronics store.

Billy: I'm in.

Melinda: Hold on, just to be clear here, you want us to help you traffic weapons this weekend?

Billy: Hubert, there will be hot girls there, right?

Hubert: I dunno, yeah, probably.

Billy: I'm willing to risk it.

Hubert: And to be honest, Melinda, no, I don't want you two anywhere near Sophia.

Billy: Why not?

Hubert: The number of reasons boggles the mind, but the main one is that at some point you're bound to ruin my chances with her.

Billy: Don't worry, Hubert, I'm sure you're fully capable of ruining those chances yourself. (to Melinda) So, you in?

Melinda: Sounds like a hippie fest to me.

Hubert: Fine, don't go. I'll tell Sophia you're sick or something.

Melinda: I'll go, for two reasons. Number one, to fluster you, Hubert. Number two, to get more FBI money. Make sure Clapper pays us for this, Hubert.

Billy: Oh, yeah, speaking of which, where's our money for taping your little TSA fiasco?
Hubert: I've been procrastinating.

Melinda: Not interested in collecting your money?

Hubert: No, not that. Just trying to avoid Clapper as much as possible.

Hubert's phone starts buzzing.

Hubert (answers call): Speak of the devil.

Clapper: Aw, Hubert, you really know just what to say to flatter an FBI guy. Anyway, look out the front entrance!

Hubert (craning neck to look out the glass doors): You're here? Why don't you just come in?

Clapper: New regulations. I can't meet you guys inside your day job anymore.

Hubert (huffing): Unreal. Ok, I'll be right there.

Hubert walks out.

Clapper: I've got a little package in the car for ya!

They start walking through the parking lot.

Hubert: So while you're here, I might as well tell ya that I'm going to a big social function with Sophia this weekend, and I think Billy and Melinda are coming, too.

Clapper: That's great! She's going to some dark enclave to further plot the anarchist agenda?

Hubert (cringing): That might be the most insane thing I've ever heard.

They arrive at Clapper's car. Clapper pulls out a huge, neon pink suitcase from the trunk.

Clapper: There ya go!

Hubert: What the hell is that?

Clapper: A suitcase.

Hubert: I know that, but what do you want me to do with it?

Clapper: It's got your money in it. All ones, just the way ya like it. Make sure I get the case back, though.

Hubert: That's not the way I like it!

Clapper: Had me fooled.

Hubert: That doesn't take much. Anyway, we'll get paid for this weekend's trip, right?

Clapper: If you produce valuable intel, then yeah. Tell me all ya know now, though.

Hubert: All I know is it's like a festival and kind of a swap meet, I guess.

Clapper: And what's your girl bringing to swap?

Hubert: Guns.

Clapper (goes berserk): What?! Guns!? OH, man, this is big. Yeah, you go, Hubert, all three of you. I want everything recorded, in triplicate! Wow! Guns!

Hubert: Ok, I gotta go. Next time pay with an envelope of hundreds, ok?

Clapper: I'll see what I can do.

Scene 3

Clapper is meeting his boss, Mr. Prick, at FBI headquarters. Mr. Prick is seated at his desk, puffing aggressively on a fat cigar.

Clapper: Sir, has the smoking ban been lifted in the building?

Mr. Prick: Dammit, Clapper! (slams fist on desk) Don't you get smart with me!

Clapper: Sorry, sir.

Mr. Prick: So tell me, what's this big news you're so giddy about?

Clapper: Well, sir, Hubert and his Nerd Squad associates might have a huge breakthrough. They're going to some hippie festival, sir, and the girl Sophia is apparently going to sell a large number of guns.

Mr. Prick: Guns and hippies! Dammit, Clapper! That is a scary thought!

Clapper: I thought you might feel that way, sir.

Mr. Prick (slams fist on desk again, puffs cigar, coughs):
Dammit, Clapper! There you go, trying to think again! What did I tell you about that?!

Clapper: Yes, sir.

Mr. Prick: Now here's what I want from you, Clapper! While Sophia is gone this weekend, I want you to get into her dirty little den of disobedience and you dig deep! I want every little nook and cranny detail documented, copied, analyzed, taped, and scraped!

Clapper (confused): Scraped, sir?

Mr. Prick: Dammit, Clapper! What did I tell you about interrupting me!?

Clapper: Yes, sir.

Mr. Prick: Do you think you can handle this mission, Clapper?!

Clapper: Of course, sir.
Mr. Prick: That's great, Clapper! Just one more thing.

Clapper; Yes, sir.

Mr. Prick: Just don't get caught! If you get caught and expose our objectives, then I and a team of mercenaries will be forced to destroy your pathetic life! Nothing personal, of course.

Clapper: You can count on me, sir. (stands up to leave)

Mr. Prick: Oh, just one more thing. Bring me an Irish Coffee from Bill's across the street!

Clapper: Yes, sir!
Mr. Prick: Make that a double!

Scene 4

Hubert, Sophia, Billy, and Melinda have arrived at the event's location, a large, serene place in the wooded mountains. Lots of activity is buzzing all around them as others are arriving and preparing for the weekend. They're busy setting up 3D printed mini-cabins. Sophia's rented van is loaded down with guns.

Melinda: So, that's the most guns ever.

Sophia (chipper): Yeah, cool, right?

Billy: No way you can sell out in one weekend.

Sophia: Wanna bet?

Billy: Sure, I bet you a romantic dinner for two.

Sophia: Nice try.

Hubert: Are you sure this is legal? It doesn't seem legal.

Sophia: It's moral, so it isn't wrong.

Melinda: So Hubert, what are you selling this weekend?

Billy: He's selling his pale, underdeveloped body.

Sophia (horrified): You guys are horrible.

A guy stops by the van, dressed in full Muslim religious attire.

Hubert (pointing at guy, whispering): Hey, Sophia, is that a Muslim?
Sophia (looking at van): Yep. Why are you whispering? (recognizes the guy) Oh, hey, Muhamed! Hey!
Muhamed (looks towards Sophia): Ah, Sophia! I should have known it was you! This is your van, right?

Sophia: Yes it is! Ya interested?

Muhamed: Yeah, you always have good quality. How about a round trip flight, max 1000 miles as a donation?

Sophia: Sounds good to me!

Muhamed (gets out smart phone): I'll send you the contract voucher now.

Sophia: Awesome. Go ahead and take your pick!

Muhamed grabs a gun, says goodbye, and walks off.

Melinda: What just happened?

Sophia: Free trade. Peaceful, voluntary interaction. He's a great guy. I've known him for years.

Melinda: But he's Muslim.

Sophia: He practices the religion of Islam, yes.

Billy: That doesn't bother you?

Sophia: No, why?

123

Hubert: Because he's Muslim.

Sophia: That has nothing to do with if I want to interact with someone. Now if he were a cop or a soldier, I'd never associate with him. But Muslim? Not a problem.

Hubert, Billy, and Melinda stare awkwardly at Sophia.

Sophia: What?

Billy: I'm gonna go try and find a beer.

Melinda: I'm with ya!

Scene 5

Richard Clapper is desperately trying to pick the lock of Sophia's front door.

Clapper (talking to himself): It's been so long since I picked a lock. At least two weeks, since the last time I locked myself out of my house. (starts grunting, frustration mounting) Come on you little!

He glances around to make sure the coast is clear, then kicks the door in. Two steps into the apartment and he sets off a motion sensor, which starts the security system to record from multiple angles and also initiates a robot controlled dart-gun. A sedative-tipped dart fires and scores a direct hit into Clapper's neck. He instantly passes out. An automated intruder alert is sent to Sophia's phone.

Back at the Donation Market Event....

Sophia (glances at phone): Uh, oh!

Hubert: I know, I didn't get that wall up perfectly straight. I'll fix it.

Sophia: No, not that. My house got broken into!

Hubert: Oh, I'm so sorry.

Sophia (upset, holding phone up to Hubert's face): Any idea why your Uncle Clapper would be breaking in?

Hubert stares with stunned look on face at the live video feed on Sophia's phone.

End Episode 12

Episode 13

Scene 1

Hubert is shocked, staring at the video feed of an unconscious Clapper on Sophia's floor.

Sophia (angry): So, what's the deal? Why is your FBI uncle breaking into my house?

Hubert (sweating): I don't know what to say.

Sophia: That makes two of us.

Hubert: I'm sure he wouldn't be there in his FBI capacity.

Sophia: And in what capacity might he be there, hmmmm? Is he Cosa Nostra? A Crip, a Blood?

Hubert: No, he's not a gang member.

Sophia: Other than the biggest gang on earth. The state gang.

Hubert: Well, ya see, there's something else about my uncle that I should tell you.

Sophia (hands on hips): I'm waiting!

Hubert: He's a klepto.

Sophia: Excuse me?

Hubert: A kleptomaniac.

Sophia (doubtful): Really.

Hubert: Yeah, we used to call him Uncle Klep. He'd always steal something when he came to visit. Nothing big, just something small, ya know, like a paper clip.

Sophia: Well, it kind of makes sense. After all, the FBI uses all stolen funds.

Melinda and Billy come back, very happy, with an assortment of goods, including some home made beer.

Melinda: This place is awesome!

Hubert: We're leaving.

Billy: You would ruin this for us.

Sophia: Why are we leaving? I'm not leaving.

Melinda: Why are you leaving, Hubert, if she's not leaving?

Hubert: Ok, I'm confused.

Billy (to Sophia): This happens to him at an alarming rate. You've been warned.

Hubert: Hold on. Sophia, don't you have to go home and handle that situation?

Billy: If this situation is Hubert's fault, I say he goes to fix it, and Sophia can stay.

Sophia: My security system can handle it.

Hubert (uncomfortable): Ummm, could you be more specific?

Sophia: My security system. Once your uncle klepto FBI creep, or whatever he is, wakes up, he'll have 15 seconds to leave. If he's smart, he'll leave and everything will be finished.

Hubert: He's not too bright. So what'll happen if he doesn't leave in 15 seconds?

Sophia: He'll get sedated again. It'll keep happening indefinitely until I shut the system down.

Melinda: Could somebody fill me in here?

Hubert: Clapper broke into Sophia's place.

Billy: And you have a security system that automatically neutralizes intruders?

Sophia: Yep.

Billy: I'm enamored. Can you take care of me forever?

Sophia: Ew!

Hubert: Billy!

Sophia's phone beeps.

Sophia: Oh, he just woke up!

Billy: 100 bucks says he's not smart enough to get out!

Melinda (casually sipping beer): No takers.

Clapper stands up, scratches head, yawns, and looks around.

Clapper: What's that beeping?
Clapper is then hit with another sedative-tipped dart and he flops to the floor.

Hubert cringes and sighs.

Hubert: Um, are you sure you should do this to an FBI agent? I mean, can't ya just let him go? I'll chastise him the next time I see him.

Billy (sarcastic): Yeah, Sophia, let big Hubert handle it for ya. He's real intimidating. All 120 pounds of him.

Sophia: He's a regular person, just like anyone else. Just because he carries a badge doesn't give him special rights. The bottom line is, he's doing something wrong, and I'm defending my rights and property. Anyway, enough! Let's go have some fun! Hubert, you can help me sell the guns.

Hubert: How?

Sophia (sarcastic): I'll use you for target practice.

Scene 2

2 days later at Nerd Squad headquarters, Hubert is calling Clapper.

Clapper (groggy, rubbing head gingerly): Clapper here.

Hubert (nonchalant): Hey Clapper. How was your weekend?

Clapper: Oh, ya know, the usual.

Hubert (sarcastic): Really? Breaking and entering is your preferred weekend activity?

Clapper (playing dumb): Whatever do you mean?

Hubert: Come on Clapper! We saw you break into Sophia's apartment! What the hell were you doing?

Clapper: Just following orders. And how the hell do you know?

Hubert: Cuz the system that kept you drooling on the carpet was also sending a live video feed to Sophia. It got so bad that people were actually making substantial bets on the whole fiasco!

Clapper (nervous): Really? Ok, ok, ya got me! Let's keep this between the two of us, ok?

Hubert: Not possible. Melinda and Billy were with us.

Clapper: Ok, then, between the four of us.

Hubert: Why?

Clapper: Well, getting caught wasn't part of the plan, and let's just say my boss is allergic to bad news. Anyway, how was the hippie fest? You get some good intel? Sell all those guns?

Hubert: Ok, not a hippie fest. Yes, all the guns were sold. We had a great time. No intel for you.

Clapper: Do you wanna get paid or not?

Hubert: Oh, you'll pay me, intel or not.

Clapper: OH, and just why is that?

Hubert (smug): I'll tell your boss about the whole thing.

Clapper: You can't blackmail me!
Hubert: Why not?

Clapper: Cuz I'll tell Sophia that you've been spying on her.

Hubert: You won't do that.

Clapper: Why not?

Hubert: Cuz I'm your best contact with Sophia.

Clapper: Ok, nerd, you win. Well played. You really are FBI material! I wasn't blackmailing at such a young age!

Hubert (annoyed): Goodbye, Clapper.

Melinda and Billy walk in.

Hubert: Hi guys.

Melinda: Hi Hubert. Where's my money?

Hubert: You guys had a great time this weekend. Isn't that enough?

Billy: Hubert, you saying that with a straight face leads me to believe that you're not joking.

Hubert (thoughtful look): Wasn't it amazing, all that stuff at the festival. I mean, most of the trade was done without dollars, and some of it was even done without money. And there were no police. And no violence. Even the road was private!

Billy (to Melinda): Is this a sly tactic he's devised to not pay us?

Melinda: He's not that clever.

Hubert (wistful look): Hmmm, guys, I'm having a revelation. What if we don't need gov….

Berry cuts Hubert off.

Berry: HEY! Looks like a slow day today. I'm going over to Happy's for day drinks! Any takers?

Billy (excited, walking towards exit): Day drinking on the clock? You're a good boss, Berry. I don't care what Hubert says.

Billy, Melinda, and Berry leave. Hubert sighs deeply and facepalms.

Scene 3

Richard Clapper is meeting his FBI boss Mr. Prick in Mr. Prick's office.

Mr. Prick: All right, Clapper. What did you find in that peacemonger Sophia's apartment?

Clapper: Uh, well sir, I spent most of my time there doing a very thorough examination of her security system.

Mr. Prick: Is there high technology involved, Clapper?

Clapper: Yes, quite efficient, automated, effective. Very interesting technology, sir.

Mr. Prick: Dammit, Clapper! (slams fist on desk) I knew it! One of those self-defense type people! And with high technology to boot! That's the government's damn job, Clapper! And do you know what would happen if people start defending themselves?!

Clapper: Uh, gee, sir, I dunno. Ya got me.

Mr. Prick: Dammit, Clapper! Are you capable of thinking?

Clapper: You always tell me not to think, sir.

Mr. Prick: Dammit, Clapper! That's right! Anyway, if people can defend themselves, then they might learn that they don't need government! And then there goes my pension! (slams fist on desk)

Clapper: An unspeakable tragedy, sir!

Mr. Prick: Now what about the report from the Nerd Squad's weekend excursion to that peacemongering fest! I need info!

Clapper (hesitant): Um, well sir, unfortunately the Nerd Squad's intel is, uh, well, somewhere between sketchy and non-existent.

Mr. Prick (slams fist on desk): Dammit, Clapper! I think I know what the problem is!

Clapper: You do, sir?

Mr. Prick: You are!

Clapper: Yes, sir. (scratches head) How exactly am I the problem, sir?

Mr. Prick: Don't get smart with me Clapper! You're obviously not paying them enough! They lack motivation! I want you to double their payoffs!

Clapper: Double their payoffs?

Mr. Prick: Don't make me repeat myself!

Clapper: Yes, sir. I'll get on it immediately! (gets up to leave) Anything else, sir?

Mr. Prick: Yeah, a jumbo dog with extra relish. The cart should be outside by now.

Clapper: Yes, sir!

Mr. Prick: Make that two! Yelling at you takes a lot out of me!

Clapper: Yes, sir!

End Episode 13

Episode 14

Scene 1

Hubert is knocking on Sophia's door.

Sophia (sad): Hey, Hubert.

Hubert: Hey. Did I come at a bad time?

Sophia: Nah, it's fine. Come on in.

They walk in and sit on the sofa.

Hubert: So whatsup?

Sophia: My sister has banned me from speaking to my nephew…..again.

Hubert: I can relate.

Sophia: You can?

Hubert: Sure, I get banned from places sometimes.

Sophia (raised eyebrows): Right….Anyway, I've been trying to convince my nephew to drop out of school.

Hubert (surprised): Really? Why would you do that?

Sophia: Cuz school is like a prison for young people. All they do is get trained into habits and behaviors by social engineers.   I just don't want my nephew to get hurt anymore.

Hubert: Well, you finished school, didn't you? And you didn't turn out so terribly bad, right?

Sophia: Gee, thanks.

Hubert: I mean better than terrible.

Sophia: Remove foot from mouth now…..but yeah, I get what you're trying to say. I didn't finish school, though. I dropped out when I was 16.

Sophia's phone gives an alert.

Sophia (looks at message excitedly): I gotta run, Hubert. I'll explain later.

Scene 2

Sophia is approaching a scene of a car accident in a quiet suburban neighborhood. Two guys are waiting next to their cars, still inspecting damage. Sophia approaches.

Sophia: You guys called for an arbitrator on the Voluntary Arbitration app?

Guy 1: He did. I reluctantly agreed. I figure it's better than getting careless cops and insurance claws involved.

Sophia: Ok, before we start, with your permission, I'll start recording on my phone.

After an hour of listening to both their stories, estimating the damage, searching for witnesses in nearby houses, and negotiating what both feel would be a fair settlement, Sophia gives her decision.

Sophia: So that's it guys. You both have 24 hours to voluntarily accept the terms to this dispute resolution. If you decide not to accept the terms, you won't be charged.

Scene 3

Billy is having a meeting with FBI agent Richard Clapper in a Toys 'R' Plus parking lot.

Billy: This is your idea of a clandestine meeting spot?

Clapper: Sure! Who would suspect two rough and tumble FBI dudes like us meeting here. It's the perfect cover!

Billy: The more you talk, the less I want anything to do with you.

Clapper: I'm doubling your salary.

Billy: I should insult you more often. What gives?

Clapper: Have you noticed Hubert acting a little weird lately?

Billy: You mean the Hubert I work with at Nerd Squad?

Clapper: Of course. How many Huberts do you know? (gasps) Does Hubert have a body double?

Billy: Your extreme paranoid delusions lead me to believe that you have very innovative ways to beat psychological testing.

Clapper: You've got a lot to learn, kid. Everybody at the FBI is delusional.

Billy gives sideways glance.

Clapper: Anyway, about Hubert. He hasn't been feeding us too much info about his neighbor Sophia lately. Not only that, but if I didn't know better, I'd think that he's trying to avoid me!

Billy (sighs deeply): I can't imagine why anyone would try to avoid you. So what are you getting at?

Clapper: I want you to spy on Hubert, and make sure he hasn't gone rogue.

Billy: Why not Melinda?
Clapper: I thought about that, but if she started showing interest in him, it might get him suspicious.

Billy: Yes, I too find it suspicious when a female has interest in Hubert.

Clapper: So you'll do it?

Billy: One one condition. I choose the meeting place next time.

Scene 4

The next day at Nerd Squad headquarters in Fried Electronics store....

Melinda: What were you thinking?

Billy: What do you mean?

Melinda: You're sacrificing countless hours to watch Hubert? I don't care how much they pay me, I'd never do that. Can you think of anything more boring, demeaning, or disgusting to do with your time?

Billy: Hmmm, I didn't really think this through, I guess.

Melinda: Obviously. I mean, your life is pathetic enough without....

Billy cuts her off.

Billy: Ok, you've made your point very clear. (stares at wall thoughtfully) There's gotta be a way to do this without losing what little dignity I have left.

Melinda: Doubtful.

A while later, Hubert comes back into the office, fresh off a service job.

Berry (shouting from his private office): Hey Hubert! How'd it go at the Rudiski house this time?!

Hubert: The usual!

Berry: Kids used peanut butter again?!

Hubert: Yep! And jelly! And other foods I couldn't distinguish!

Berry: You salvage it?!

Hubert: Not even close! Computer chips aren't 3-year-old chef resistant yet! I gave her a coupon! She said she'll be in tomorrow!

Hubert walks over to his desk near Melinda and Billy.

Billy: Hubert, can I borrow your phone?

Hubert: Um, I guess. What's wrong with yours?

Billy: Long story.

Hubert: Ok, here ya go.

Billy takes phone and walks out. An hour later he comes back.

Hubert: What the hell, man?!

Billy (playing dumb): What?

Hubert (sighs): An hour? Really?

Billy: I'm a popular guy, what can I say?

Hubert : Whatever. I'm out of here. My time in this techno-dungeon is finished for today.

Billy smiles malevolently as Hubert walks out.

Melinda: What did ya do?

Billy: I'm not telling you!

Melinda: Why not?

Billy: Cuz you might use it for blackmail material, that's why.

Melinda: I already have blackmail material on you.

Billy: You do?

Melinda: Remember Chicago?

Billy: Damn, I forgot about that. All right, I bugged Hubert's phone. All his data now gets recorded by my home system.

Melinda: So your master plan is to not watch him, but just listen to him and read his texts?

Billy: You really do think I'm that simple minded, don't you?

Melinda: You've given me strong evidence to support that theory ever since we met.

Billy: Perhaps….but this is different. I'm going to make a key word program to find stuff Clapper might want.

Melinda: Like what?

Billy: Hell if I know. I mean, it's Clapper we're talking about, so it doesn't need to be much.

Melinda: Good point.

Scene 5

After leaving work, Hubert walks into Happy's Bar across the street from Fried Electronics. The owner, a big, rugged character named Happy, is tending the bar.

Happy: Hubert?! What are you doing here?

Hubert sits at the bar and slumps.

Hubert: Hey, Happy. I'm here to drink, what else?

Happy: I figured, you just hardly come in, so I'm surprised.

Hubert: Yeah, I'm having some problems, so I figured I'd stop in.

Happy: So you've joined the masses in drowning their sorrows in cheap booze, huh?

Hubert: Just for one night.

Happy points to a scuzzy guy with his drooling face planted in the bar.

Happy: That's what that guy said a few years ago.

Hubert: Shot of tequila, please.

Happy pours shot. Hubert slams it.

Happy: So what's the trouble?

Hubert: Guilty conscience.

Happy: This wouldn't have anything to do with you spying on your girlfriend, now would it?

Hubert: Girlfriend?

Happy: Sophia, right?

Hubert: She's just a friend, but yes, wait, how did you know I'm spying on her?

Happy: Everybody around here knows. (points back to the face-planter) I think even he knows.

Hubert (dejected): Great.

Happy: Why did you start spying on her in the first place?

Hubert: Cuz I was afraid to talk to her.

Happy: Cuz you're socially awkward.

Hubert: Right. Then I got approached by, wait, do you know...

Happy: Clapper? Yeah, I know. Everybody spills their guts to bartenders, ya know. It's tradition.

Hubert: So, anyway, it gave me an "in", I guess.

Happy: And now you're having regrets and you're looking for a way out.
Hubert: Yes! What do you think?

Happy: There's no way out.

Hubert sinks deeper into barstool and frowns.

Happy: But I will say this. The longer you wait, the worse it will be when you do fess up. Do you think you actually have a chance with this girl?

Hubert: Maybe, yeah, I dunno.

Happy: What's so special about her?

Hubert: She's beautiful, smart, energetic, and so unique.

Happy: Yes, it seems doubtful that she'd have interest in you, but, who knows? Stranger things have happened.

Hubert: You're not helping.

Happy: How is she unique?

Hubert: Well, she's involved in I dunno how many business ventures and doesn't pay any income tax.

Happy: I like her already. Hubert, why don't you just quit the FBI gig?

Hubert: Cuz I need the money.

Happy: I can't tell ya what to do, Hubert, but I've got an idea to keep your gig, but not spy on Sophia anymore. Why don't you just feed the FBI a bunch of bull? Hell, if you do it well enough, they might even get off your girlfriend's back.

Hubert: Happy! You're a genius!

Hubert's phone rings. It's Sophia. He invites her to Happy's. A short while later, she arrives and sits next to Hubert.

Happy: Wow, look at you. Welcome to Happy's. I'm Happy.

Sophia: Thanks! I'm Sophia.

Happy: Why are you with Hubert?
Hubert: I can hear you, ya know.

Sophia: Hubert, I want to apologize for running out on you so fast yesterday.

Hubert: No problem. Where'd you go?

Sophia: Glad you asked! I just joined this private arbitration company and got my first gig as an arbitrator! I got paid in crypto!

Happy: Private arbitration?

Sophia: Yeah, people who want to settle disputes, but don't want to deal with the hassle, incompetence, and inefficiencies of the ridiculous state monopoly.

Happy: You sound pretty smart. Again, why Hubert?

Sophia: 2 tequilas, please! Do you take crypto?

Happy: I have a wine cellar, but no crypts.

Hubert: Not what she meant. Do you take Bitcoin or Bitcoin Cash or anything like that?

Happy: Is that English?

Sophia (giggling): It's ok. They're voluntary currencies.

Happy: Are they tax free?

Sophia: They can be!

Happy: You have my attention.

Scene 6

2 days later, Billy is in his dingy apartment, plotting.

Billy (grinning malevolently, slowly twirling in office chair): Hubert, that was a very interesting talk you had with Happy. Now I just need to figure out the best way to take advantage.

End Episode 14

Episode 15

Scene 1

At Nerd Squad headquarters inside Fried Electronics store, Hubert is reading a book when Billy walks in.

Billy (skeptical look): Hubert, what are you doing?

Hubert: What does it look like?

Billy: It looks like you're reading a book, but I know you don't read anything but comics, hence my confusion.

Hubert: There are many more reasons for your confusion.

Billy (yelling towards Berry's office): Berry! Hubert's acting weird!

Berry (yelling): I'm busy!

Billy: With what?!

Berry: I'm on the verge of beating your high score on Pac-Man!

Billy (chagrined): Impossible! (sighs, turns to Hubert) Anyway, whatcha reading?

Hubert: For A New Liberty, by Murray Rothbard. Sophia recommended it.

Billy: Oh, speaking of Sophia, I couldn't help but get wind of a little talk you had the other day with Happy.

Hubert: I talked to Happy alone. How would you know that?

Billy: Come now, let's not dwell on pesky little details. Let's talk about what you said about Sophia and Clapper. You said you might feed Clapper false info about her. (wagging finger) Tisk, tisk.

Hubert: I never said that. And what are you getting at anyway?

Billy: Well, I might tell Clapper, and I might not. It's up to you and how much you're willing to pay.

Hubert: You're blackmailing me?!

Billy: I wouldn't say that, exactly.

Berry (yelling from his private office): Ha! I did it!

Billy: Kinda busy right now!

Berry: I did it! I beat your top score on Pac-Man, Billy!

Billy cringes.

Hubert: Anyway, go ahead and tell Clapper whatever you want. I don't care.

Billy (disappointed): Really? Just 50 bucks, come on.

Hubert: No.

Billy: 10 bucks.

Hubert: Way to play hardball.

Berry steps out of office.

Berry: I'm going to Happy's to have a celebratory drink and pat myself on the back. Wanna come so I can rub it in your face, Billy?

Billy (sarcastic): Very tempting.

Berry: What are you so busy with, anyway? There isn't another service call scheduled for an hour.

Billy: Blackmailing Hubert.

Berry: Hey, keep that dirty FBI blackmailing business out of here. I'm trying to run a respectable establishment. Oh, and by the way, did you get Mrs. Smith to take that software upgrade she doesn't need?

Billy: Of course.

Scene 2

Clapper is meeting Billy at a park near an elementary school.

Billy: The meeting spots you choose continuously get creepier. Why here?

Clapper (looking over shoulder in suspicious manner): Hey, I'm the FBI vet here. Don't question my methods.

Billy: Whatever. So there are some problems with Hubert. First of all, I caught him reading a book at work.

Clapper (gasps, grabs chest): It's worse than I thought! What was he reading?

Billy: I dunno, some guy named Rothbard, I think.

Clapper: Hmmm, that name sounds familiar. I think he was one of those liberty advocates from my younger days.

Billy: But that's not all. He's gonna protect Sophia by deliberately giving you bad intel.

Clapper (scratching head): Does that mean on purpose?

Billy (facepalm): Yeah, it does.

Clapper: I knew it! She's getting in his head! It's a dangerous game we play, Billy. So how'd you find that out?

Billy: I bugged his phone and he had a talk with..

Clapper cuts him off.

Clapper: Whoa! You did what?!

Billy: I bugged his phone.

Clapper: Why the hell did you do that?

Billy (shocked): Why the hell not?!

Clapper: What do you think the NSA exists for? Everything is already recorded! I don't need you to bug phones. I pay you to get intel where electronics don't reach yet. I need you to spend more time with Hubert. Engage him more. Hell, try and hang out with him and Sophia together! Do I have to tell you everything?

Billy (gulps): Spend time with Hubert? My social life just took a severe plunge.

Clapper (laughing): Social life? You?

Billy (grimacing, offended): So you have my money?

Clapper: Not this time. Gotta teach you a lesson!

Billy: Lesson?!

Clapper: Yeah, uh, don't do the NSA's job for 'em.

Billy: Sounds like a lame excuse to keep my money for yourself.

Scene 3

Sophia and Hubert are chatting at Sophia's apartment.

Sophia (excited): So check out this video I posted on Odysee!

Shows phone screen to Hubert.

Hubert: What is it?

Sophia: I did random man-in-the-street interviews. I asked people, "What is a right?".

Hubert: Did anyone get it?

Sophia: Only two out of a hundred.

Hubert: Wow, that's sad.

Sophia: Like you're one to talk. Can you define it?

Hubert (stuttering): Um, well, I guess, uh, gimme a minute.

Sophia: Uh huh. Just what I thought.

Hubert (defensive): Can you?

Sophia: Sure, it's easy. A right is any action that doesn't initiate harm to another sentient being.

Hubert (uncertain): If it were only so simple.

Sophia: It is! People just don't realize it. By the way, did you finish that Rothbard book I loaned you?

Hubert: Almost.

Sophia: What do ya think?

Hubert: Well, I think it's great in theory, but…

He gets interrupted by an alarm on Sophia's phone.

Sophia: Oh no!

Hubert: What's wrong?

Sophia: I just got an alert on my Copblock app. One of my friends is being harassed by rights-violators!

Hubert: What the heck is a rights-violator?

Sophia: A cop!

Hubert: Why do you think he's at your friend's house?

Sophia: Probably for the plants my friend grows.

Hubert: What kind of plants?

Sophia: Use your imagination. I gotta run. Ya wanna come?

Hubert (looking at the time on his phone): I'd love to, but look at the time.

Sophia: Aw, come on, live a little!

Scene 4

Hubert and Sophia approach Sophia's friend's house in the suburbs. Two cops are arguing with people on the front deck. Sophia is recording with her phone and Hubert walks behind her timidly.

Sophia: Why are you walking behind me?

Hubert: Does the term 'human shield' mean anything to you?

Sophia: Gee, thanks.

Sophia gets into the mix on the deck.

Sophia: Hey, what's going on here?

Cop: None of your business.

Person 1: This order-follower is trespassing on private property and making violent threats. (to Sophia) You from Copblock?

Sophia: Yep. (to cop) And if rights are being violated, then it is my business. It's everyone's business. So what are you doing here?

Cop: Trying to do my job.

Sophia: Why? Has the property owner done something wrong? You're the one here harassing people.

Cop (throws hands up): That's it, I'm calling for backup. (walks towards car parked lopsidedly on curb and grass) And stop filming me!

20 minutes later, there are 10 people trying to defend the rights of the homeowner, who has remained inside. All of them are sitting on the front deck and refusing to move. The cops are huddling together on the front lawn and trying to figure out what to do.

Cop 1: All I know is, the sooner we get this done, the sooner I can get to Denny's.

Sophia gets up.

Hubert (hushed tone): Sophia! What are you doing?

Sophia: Shhhh. Stay put. I wanna surprise 'em.

Sophia casually walks up close enough to pick up audio and video with her phone.

Cop 2: I say we arrest 'em all.

Sophia: You mean throw us in a cage? For doing nothing wrong? Just leave us in peace and mind your own business.

Cop 1: Ok, that's it. Let's arrest 'em, her first.

Sophia sits on grass.

Cop 1: Get up.

Sophia: I won't. (shouts back to people sitting on deck) They're gonna try and throw us in a cage!

Cop 2: Gonna do this the hard way, huh?

Cop 2 picks Sophia up, carries her, and throws her in the back seat of the extortion-funded squad car.

All of the other order-followers with badges and uniforms head to the deck, start cuffing people and carrying them to the squad cars. Hubert screams and starts crying. Order-followers laugh sadistically.

Scene 5

Clapper is having a meeting with Mr. Prick at Prick's office. Prick is sitting at his desk, leaning on it, and scowling.

Mr. Prick: Dammit, Clapper! (slams fist on desk) A book you say!

Clapper: I'm afraid so, sir.

Mr Prick: Do you know the author!?

Clapper: It was reportedly by Murray Rothbard, sir.

Mr. Prick (slams fist on desk): Dammit, Clapper! Rothbard! This is worse than I thought! That's one of the most notorious gangster families ever!

Clapper (confused): Um, excuse me, sir?

Mr. Prick: Gangster! So the anarcho-peacenik empire is teaming up with La Cosa Nostra?! This is the mother of all conspiracies, Clapper!

Clapper: Um, sir, I think you might be thinking of Rothman, not Rothbard.

Mr. Prick: Clapper! How many times have I told you not to think!? And don't interrupt when I'm yelling!

Clapper: Yes, sir.

Mr. Prick: So you think that Sophia might be turning Hubert?!

Clapper: You just told me not to think, sir.

Mr. Prick: Don't contradict me, Clapper!

Clapper: Sorry, sir. Yes, I have reason to believe that Hubert might not be completely reliable anymore.

Mr. Prick: Dammit, Clapper! You know who is to blame?!

Clapper: I dunno, sir, but I'm quite sure you do.

Mr. Prick (slams fist on desk): This is your fault, Clapper! You're his handler! It's your responsibility to control him!

Clapper: Sir, I can't really control his behavior, can I?

Mr Prick: Of course you can, Clapper! Hell, I control you, don't I? That's how hierarchies work!

Clapper: I suppose so, sir.

Mr. Prick: Then dammit, Clapper! Get on the ball! You've got to control him better so that the anarcho-peacenik-cosa nostra-book-reader conspiracy gets nipped in the bud!

Clapper: Sir, with all due respect, might you be jumping to conclusions?

Mr. Prick: Clapper! How long have you been with the FBI?! Jumping to conclusions is what keeps us in business! Well, that, and fear and ignorance.

Clapper's phone rings. Clapper continues staring intently at Mr. Prick.

Mr. Prick: The sooner you answer that, Clapper, the sooner that awful noise will stop!

Clapper answers.

Clapper: Hey Billy. I'm busy getting yelled at.

Billy: Hubert just got arrested.

End Episode 15

Episode 16

Scene 1

Hubert and Sophia are in a cage. A uniformed rights-violator approaches the cage.

Rights-violator (unlocking cage door): You two made bail!

They leave the cage, sign some morally-relativistic garbage documents under duress, and walk out to the street. Billy is waiting for them.

Sophia: You?

Billy (smug): Me. Need a ride?

Hubert (relieved): I need a lot more than a lift. That was so scary.

Sophia: OH, come on. All you did was sit in a holding cell with me for a few hours. And look all the good you did!

Billy: By getting locked up? You have a strange idea of what good is.

Sophia: He helped defend rights. And it's gonna get so much attention on Odysee! Don't you feel great!

Hubert: I feel like I need a shower and a cup of coffee.

They get into Billy's old Chevy Cavalier. He tries to start it, but it won't crank.

Billy: Damn Murphy's Law.

Sophia: No worries, I'll get one on my phone. I owe you for the bail, though, so that should more than cover a tow truck. How much?

Billy: Actually, if you're interested, I'm having a poker game tomorrow night. Instead of paying me back, how bout I just deal you in?

Sophia: Only if Hubert comes.

Billy: What do you see in him?

Hubert (offended): I'm right here, Billy! I can hear you!

Billy: Fine.

Sophia: How many players so far?

Billy: Counting myself, 3.

Scene 2

At Nerd Squad headquarters in Fried Electronics Store, Hubert is sleeping with face down on desk, and snoring loudly. Billy is reading a poker strategy guide online. Melinda walks in.

Melinda (excited): Hey Billy!

Billy (glances up from laptop): I find it unnerving when you're excited to see me.

Melinda: I got new smart shoes!

Billy: Cool. If they're so smart, they'll help you get a better job. Then I'll have some peace.

Melinda: Check this out. (takes one shoe off) I don't even have to tie it. It automatically tightens itself to my foot!

She puts the shoe back on, it tightens with zippy-sounding gusto.

Melinda: See! Perfect!

Shoe makes further adjustments and gets much tighter.

Melinda (cringing): Ow! Too tight! Too tight! Stop it!

Shoe talks: Optimum comfort level has not yet been reached. Please standby.

Billy looks on with bemusement. Starts recording with phone.

Berry (yelling from his private office): Hey! What's going on out there!?

Billy: Melinda is getting abused by overpriced shoes!

Berry hustles out of his office to take a look.

Melinda (in pain, tugging at shoe): Stop recording!

She pulls desperately to get the shoe off, and finally succeeds.

Billy: Pretty smart.

Melinda (gasping for breath): I don't wanna hear it, Billy.

Billy: I usually like to give any new product a year on the market before I trust it. Always some bugs to work out. You should know. We work with Mycrosoft crap all day.

Melinda (angry sarcasm): Yeah, well, good for you, Billy.

Billy: How much did you pay for those anyway?

Hubert wakes up, startled.

Billy: Hubert, you miss all the good stuff.

Berry: Hubert, it's not like you to sleep on the job. That's Billy's department. What gives?

Billy: He got arrested.

Hubert: Billy!

Berry (amused): Really?

Billy: Yep, he spent all night in the slammer with Sophia.

Melinda: Does Clapper know?

Hubert: No, and I'd like to keep it that way.

Billy (winks at Hubert): You can count on me.

Hubert: I don't get why people think that winking is comforting.

Billy: Berry, you game to lose some of your ill-gotten cash tonight? Poker? My place? Or you still sore from last time?

Berry: What are you talking about? You still haven't paid me what you owe me from last time.

Billy: Very well, looks like the house will have to float you credit.

Berry: All right, I'm in, but you'd better pay up this time.

Billy: Melinda, you in?

Melinda (rubbing foot): I hang out with you creeps enough here at work.

Billy: Come on, it's a better investment than those shoes. Sophia's coming!

Melinda: Well, I guess if she's gonna be there. I wouldn't mind taking your money anyway.

Hubert's phone rings. Hubert sees that it's Clapper and frowns.

Hubert: Hey Clapper.

Clapper: Hubert! I'm outside!

Hubert: Congratulations.

Clapper: Step out so we can have a talk.

Hubert: Can't you just come in here?

Clapper: I could, but I don't want Billy to see me.

Hubert: He knows you're here.

Clapper: Just come out!

Hubert hangs up and goes outside to meet Clapper in the parking lot.

Clapper: Hey, haven't heard from you in a while! Anything new to report?

Hubert (eyes dart, feet shuffle awkwardly): Nope, pretty normal. Totally normal life. Haven't done anything out of the ordinary lately.

Clapper: Really? You haven't talked to Sophia?

Hubert: Nah, not much. She does her thing, I do mine.

Clapper (tilts head and smirks): Is that right? Ok, well, just let me know when something comes up, ok?

Hubert (fake smile): Sure thing.

5 minutes later, Billy gets a text from Clapper....

WE NEED TO TALK

Scene 3

The next day, Billy sets up a spy camera in his living room.

And later that night, Billy, Melinda, and Berry are sipping cheap beer on the patio when Sophia and Hubert pull up in the driveway. Sophia and Hubert approach the patio.

Sophia: Nice place.

Billy: Don't patronize me. You know where I work.

Hubert groans.

30 minutes later, all five are seated around a rickety card table. Eighties pop music plays in the background. Sophia already has a sizable advantage in chips.

Sophia: Full house.

Berry (throws cards down in disgust): Again! Something ain't right here. Are you a professional gambler?

Billy: I'm a professional gambler.

Hubert: You're a degenerate gambler, Billy. Big difference.

Sophia: I hardly play.

Berry: That doesn't make me feel better.

Hubert: Billy's the one reading strategy guides and losing, so don't feel too bad.

Berry: What do you do for a living, Sophia?

Sophia: I eat, sleep, breathe. All the stuff other people do.

Hubert: She writes, and trades crypto, and makes 3D printed stuff and sells it.

Sophia: Yep, tax free, too!

Berry: What do you mean, tax free?

Sophia: I don't pay any extortion fees to the criminal gang called the IRS.

Billy: But you file, right?

Sophia: Nope.

Berry: Aren't you afraid of, well.....

Sophia: Getting robbed at gunpoint or thrown in a cage by ignorant, IRS goons? Nope. If ya want freedom, ya gotta take it, so that's what I do.

Berry: So what got you and Hubert in the slammer the other day?

Sophia: We were blocking rights-violators in uniforms from entering my friend's house. They wanted to steal my friend's Cannabis plants and throw him in a cage.

Billy: Your friend has a prescription or something?

Sophia: Nope, just natural freedom like the rest of us.

Berry: You're gutsy, I like that. How about I fire Melinda and you come work for me?

Melinda: Hey!

Sophia (rolls eyes): Tempting.

Berry: Well, getting arrested is no big deal. Heck, if you can believe it, I got arrested once myself!

Billy (cackling): You? What did ya do? Get a ticket for balding too fast?

Berry: Ya see, back in my college days, a neighbor called the cops on me.

Melinda (sarcastic): A wild party, no doubt.

Berry: I was playing Space Invaders so damn loud that my neighbor called the cops.

Sophia: And rather than try to talk to you, they just called the gang in blue?

Berry: Well, I can't be certain, cuz it really was so loud. Hell, when the cops showed up, I didn't even hear them until they bashed the dang door down!

Hubert: I suddenly feel somewhat shameful for having you as a boss.

Billy: Suddenly?

Scene 4

Later that week, Hubert meets Clapper in a Bedding, Bathing, and Way Beyond parking lot.

Hubert: You literally try to come up with the worst clandestine meeting spots, don't you? Admit it.

Clapper (loud and defensive): This is the last place people would expect two FBI studs to be meeting, so actually, it is quite the clandestine spot!

People passing by give awkward glances.

Clapper: Anyway, I've got big news. I'm pulling you off the Sophia case.

Hubert (stunned): What?! Why?!

Clapper: I'm glad you asked! She's going to be audited by the IRS. So that means her case is out of our hands, for now.

Hubert faints.
End Season 1

Check out The Evolution Saga five part scifi series by Todd Borho

James Bong – Agent of Anarchy

The C.A. Salt Project

SeAgora – A High Seas Adventure

The Great Agora Space Race

Agora One – A Space Adventure

Get more at *toddborho.com*

Made in United States
Troutdale, OR
08/29/2025